John Scott Abernethy

The Life and Work of James Abernethy

past president of the Institution of civil engineers

John Scott Abernethy

The Life and Work of James Abernethy
past president of the Institution of civil engineers

ISBN/EAN: 9783337094966

Printed in Europe, USA, Canada, Australia, Japan

Cover: Foto ©Raphael Reischuk / pixelio.de

More available books at **www.hansebooks.com**

THE

LIFE AND WORK

OF

JAMES ABERNETHY, C.E., F.R.S.E.

Yrs faithfully
Jas Abernethy

THE
LIFE AND WORK

OF

JAMES ABERNETHY, C.E.

F.R.S.E.

Past President of the Institution of Civil Engineers.

BY HIS SON,

JOHN S. ABERNETHY, M.A. (Oxon.)

BARRISTER-AT-LAW.

Bid harbours open, public ways extend,
Bid the broad arch the dangerous flood contain,
The mole projected break the roaring main,
Back to his bounds the subject sea command,
And roll obedient rivers through the land.
These honours peace to happy Britain brings,
These are imperial works, and worthy kings

POPE, "MORAL ESSAYS," Epist. iv., 197—204.

London:

T. BRETTELL & CO., PRINTERS, RUPERT STREET, W

1897.

Seven Shillings and Sixpence.

PREFACE.

————◄•►————

THE author has endeavoured to give in the pages which follow a concise review of the long life of his late father, and some account of the principal works designed and executed by him in the United Kingdom and Abroad.

These, it is hoped, will long remain as visible proofs of his industry and ability as a Harbour and Dock Engineer now that his life has closed, but as in the opinion of many friends he was scarcely so well known to his countrymen outside the pale of the Civil Engineering Profession while living, as was justified by his works, the author has felt himself called upon to record them in a Biography, and thus enable all who so desire to read of him and of his professional career at their leisure.

Moreover, the requisite materials were easily procurable from numerous diaries, and more particularly from a manuscript written shortly before his death, in which he had himself noted down the incidents he could recall, and the chief works upon which he had been engaged. With these valuable guides—easily followed by one who had enjoyed a long and close association with him—the author has been enabled to investigate and supplement from old Report and Letter Books from 1840 to the date of his decease on March 8th, 1896, all that was referred to in the manuscript, and to add such additional incidents as may be of interest from the various sources of research, and so gradually to accomplish the pleasant duty he had undertaken.

In conclusion, he trusts that no further credit is claimed for the subject of the Biography than is justly due to him. If his individuality is in any instance too prominent, there is a total absence of intention of passing over any one whose name should have been mentioned in connection with any of the particular engineering works described. Any such error, either in commission or omission, would be a course of regret to

THE AUTHOR.

4, Delahay Street,
Westminster, S.W.
July, 1897.

CONTENTS.

LIST OF ILLUSTRATIONS.

———◇———

EARLY DAYS.

THE name Abernethy is stated in Douglas' "History of the Scottish Peerage," to be "of great antiquity," and to "have made a considerable figure in Scotland before surnames were used, and though it is evident that there was no peerage in the family till Lawrence Abernethy,* of Salton, was created a Lord of Parliament by King James the Second (King of Scotland, 1436—1460, *temp*. Henry VI. of England) yet historians have always looked upon them in this rank on account of the considerable place they had among the chief barons."

The progenitor of the Abernethys was Orm (lay Abbot of Abernethy, in Perthshire, A.D. 596) the son of Hugh, who flourished under Malcolm IV., several of whose charters he witnessed, and possessed during

---

* Lawrence Abernethy of Salton, and Rothemay 11th in descent from Orm (lay Abbot of Abernethy, in Perthshire, in 1164), was created a Peer on June 28th, 1445.

B

this reign the lands of Innerloppie, in Forfarshire,
and Balbrennie, in Fife.   From William Malcolm's
successor he acquired the Manor of Abernethy, in
Strathern, and from this Manor, Orm and his son
Lawrence assumed the surname of Abernethy on June
28th, 1164.

The family, one of the oldest in Scotland, was also,
according to Winten, one of the original three who
shared in the transcendent *privilege of sanctuary*,—

> "That is ye blak Prest of Weddale,
>   The Thane of Fyfe, and ye thryd syne,
>   Quhalwyre be Lord of Abbyrnethyne."

These passages, quoted from the above named
authorities on "Peerage," and which are but ancil-
lary to a complete lineage given by them in the direct
line from the time of David I., King of Scotland,
who died A.D. 1150, to the ninth Lord of Salton
Alexander Abernethy, after whose death, the names
Abernethy and Fraser became merged in one Barony,
are not quoted by the author, with the intention
of drawing in outline a large tree of descent in
rivalry to the many, who have, with more or less
success, already produced specimens, on the top
branches of which (genealogical trees having the
peculiarity of growing downwards), the name of the
Conqueror is occasionally to be detected ; but rather

with the object of establishing a clear title on behalf
of the subject of this biography to be called a Scotchman
by descent, apart from the circumstances of Aberdeen*
(the City upon the mouth of the Dee) being his native
city, the city of his boyhood, and the city to which
he was destined to be recalled in early manhood, and
to reside for ten years executing his first important
work as a civil engineer. Before concluding the reference to the antiquity of the name Abernethy, it may
be allowable to pause for a moment to point out the
somewhat remarkable conservatism with which
Christian names have been preserved among members of a family, who, for a long period, perhaps now
in some instances, at an end, have continued to style
themselves Whigs, from the time that term arose in the
seventeenth century, by quoting this extract from a
Charter under the Great Seal in 1468. The Charter

---

* Aber and Inver were both used by the Southern Picts, though
not quite in the same way. Inver being generally at the mouth of
a river.—Aber at the ford usually at some distance from the mouth.
Invernethy is at the junction of the Nethy with the Earn, and Abernethy
a mile farther up the river. Skene's " Celtic Scotland " vol i., p. 222.
Nethy=neith, a turning or whirling stream. - Lewis' Topographical
Dictionary of Scotland. Mr. Isaac Taylor, in " Words and Places,"
draws a supposed line from Inverary to Aberdeen, and says the Invers
are found to the north, and the Abers south of this line, but the true
distribution of these two words north of the Firth of Forth and Clyde
is in Argyllshire, Invers alone in Invernesshire and Rosshire, Invers
and Abers in the proportion of three to one and two to one, and on the
south side of the proposed line they occur in about equal proportions
See Skene's " Celtic Scotland," vol. i., p. 221.

referred to and given at length by Douglas, and other writers on British Peerage, was granted to William Abernethy, with the following entail :—

"First to himself and the heirs male of his own body, which failing, to James Abernethy, then to George, then to Archibald, his brother german, then to his cousin, John Abernethy."

All these names, with the exception of Archibald, appear to have been studiously maintained for many generations in this branch of the family, the Abernethys of Auchinacloich, while the three last generations, as well as the present, each contain three sons bearing the Christian names above given, James being the name of the eldest son, while the father, grandfather, and great grandfather of the celebrated surgeon John Abernethy, of the Abernethys of Croskie, respectively, bore the christian name John.

One family failing, in times happily long since passed, which can, if necessary, be more easily and clearly proved than the family lineage, was the indulgence of a disposition to take part in clan warfare, and unfortunately, on the greater number of occasions, as results plainly show, to have done so on the wrong side, viewed from the point of success, notably in the case of joining the Pretender's Army in 1845-6, for which mistaken display of patriotism several of the more responsible of their representatives justly or unjustly forfeited their landed estates, and some of them their lives, and their descendants in these times can but reflect on the past family history in the plaintive lines of Lord Byron :--

> " Ill starred, though brave, did no visions foreboding
> Tell you that Fate had forsaken your cause ?
> Ah ! were you destin'd to die at Culloden,
> Victory crowned not your fall with applause."

The great grandfather of James Abernethy, some account of whose life and work will be found in the pages which follow, fell at the battle of Culloden, April 16th, 1746, while his grandfather having been deprived of his landed property removed from Newbiggin, near the parish of Abernethy, which is situated partly in Perthshire and partly in Fifeshire, and resided on a small estate Lochgellie near Kirkcaldy, in the latter county. He died at a comparatively early age, leaving a widow and four sons—James, of Ferry Hill, Aberdeen; John, a Minister of Bolton Manse, Haddington; Robert, Steward to the Hon. Col. Ford Belfast; and George an Engineer.

The subject of this biography was the eldest son of the last named by his marriage with Miss Isabella Johnston, of Nigg, near Aberdeen, daughter of Lieut. Johnston, R.N., and was born on June 12th, 1814, in the City of Aberdeen, whither his parents had removed a short time previously from Fifeshire, and one of his earliest recollections was the interest with which as a child he used to watch his father making various mechanical designs in the evenings at home, and putting them into the more tangible form of wood patterns in the daytime in a workshop adjoining the house.

The whaling ships at the foot of Marischal Street, with their oily cargoes and jaw bones of the gigantic mammals which had furnished them, suspended from the rigging as trophies, and perchance calculated to attract some passing observer as being a fanciful sub-stitute for wooden gate-posts as an entrance to his suburban garden, were equally objects of attraction, and induced him to pay frequent visits to the then small tidal harbour in the bed of the River Dee, where an island known as "The Inches" separated the river from the harbour on the north side of it, and where some twenty years later he commenced his first impor-tant work as a civil engineer, while the Links, the Braid Hill, the "Auld Toon," with its cathedral, and the Brig of Balgownie by the River Don comprised some of the selected localities for early days' pedes-trianism.

> " Often I think of the beautiful town,
>   That is seated by the sea,
>   Often in thought go up and down.
>   The pleasant streets of that dear old town,
>   And my youth comes back to me."

But the above enumeration did not apparently ex-
haust the scenes of daily rambles, for it is recorded
that on a certain occasion while wheeling a barrow in
too close proximity to the canal bank, he lost his
balance and fell upon the towing path below, breaking
his right arm at the elbow, besides other minor damages.
Dr. Blaikie, who had formerly been an army surgeon,
carefully set the fractured limb, but the bandages were
released prematurely, resulting in a false joint in the
elbow, and the right arm considerably longer than the
left. The accident, however, had its fortunate effects
as well, for it tended to an increase of strength
in the limb, and he used to remark, "I found it
advantageous in my after school-day combats."

Of the citizens resident in Aberdeen before the year
1823 he has recorded in writing his recollection of Mr.
and Mrs. Milne, whose school in King Street, he
attended : James Davidson, a thread manufacturer,
who resided at a house situated at the end of a passage
leading from North Street to King Street, to whose
grandchildren's parties he was at times invited, and
whom he met some years later on the point of emigra-
ting to the United States, broken in fortune, but not
in spirit ; and a Mr. Morgan, a retired West Indian
planter, who lived a short distance out of the city, and
who kept what is popularly termed an open house, at
which one of his chief amusements was to invite

certain of the hardier headed and better seasoned
citizens to partake of rum punch in the evenings, with
the result that his guests were often permitted to
depart homewards in the "sma' hours" with indistinct
topographical ideas as to the direction in which their
respective houses lay.

At the age of nine, however, a complete change of
scene with entirely new associations was in store, in
consequence of his father having obtained the post of
manager in the Iron Works of Mr. Josiah John Guest
at Dowlais in Glamorganshire, and in the summer of
1823 he embarked with his parents on a steamboat,
named the *Velocity*, which, with a sister ship, the
Brilliant, plied on alternate sailing days between Aberdeen and Leith on a voyage to the latter port, thence
the long coach journey was commenced, the route
taken being *via* Carlisle and Preston to Liverpool,
where the Mersey was crossed in a rowing boat to
Birkenhead, on the Cheshire side, at that time little
more than a village, and thence again by coach *via*
Chester and Hereford to Dowlais. A lasting impression was produced on the boy's mind by the sight
of the long extent of apple orchards through which the
coach passed in the county of Hereford, and which
were laden with fruit at the time, and another equally
permanent, though of an entirely different kind, by
the utter astonishment at seeing from his bedroom

window upon arrival at Dowlais the roaring blast furnaces and half naked forms of the puddlers dragging the red hot bars from the ovens.

Arrived at Dowlais his parents settled in a cottage at a short distance from the foundry, and attention was again paid to renewing the schooling which had been interrupted by the change of home. An old soldier, named Shaw, residing at a convenient distance, and who kept what he was pleased to style, on a signboard in front of his house, an "Academy," was selected as a suitable teacher. This "academician" was an advocate for strict discipline which he maintained through the agency of a long slender pole resembling a fishing-rod, suspended in readiness for use on hooks behind his chair, and by means of which he was enabled, without the effort of rising, to administer a corrective on the cranium of any desultory pupil within the room, an act (it was remembered) of frequent repetition during the time allotted for school hours.

The road to and from the academy lay through a prettily-wooded glen, at the bottom of which ran a clear stream, in the deeper parts of which the boys used to bathe and learn to swim, but upon a visit to the spot forty years later, all traces of glen and stream had disappeared and the site was found to be filled up with mounds of ashes and refuse from the adjoining iron works.

After a stay of some three years at Dowlais, the
acceptance by his father of a more remunerative post
as manager of a foundry in Southwark, necessitated
another family removal to London. Bristol was
reached by steamer, and thence on the following day,
seats were taken on the Regulator coach for the
metropolis; but on this particular journey, in turning
too sharply into the yard of the Swan Inn, at Newbury,
the vehicle upset, and passengers and luggage were
deposited indiscriminately and impartially on to the
stone paving. George Abernethy had the misfortune
to break an arm in the fall, which involved a postpone-
ment of the remainder of the journey for a fortnight,
at the end of which time the travellers reached their
destination at nightfall, stooping their heads under the
archway leading to the courtyard of the Belle Sauvage,
Ludgate Hill.

The locality selected for a residence was on the
Surrey side of the river, convenient to the works, and
equally eligible from the boy's point of view as being
within easy range of the menagerie at Exeter Change
and the Tower of London, at the former of which the
elephant Chunee was held in as high esteem by the
rising generation as Jumbo, half a century later at the
Zoo. He could clearly recall visits to Old London
Bridge and watching the wherries shooting the falls
between its numerous piers which remained in the river

while the new bridge was being built and long after the superstructure had been removed, and witnessed the funeral procession of the Duke of York, brother of King George IV., from the window of a surgeon's room in Knightsbridge Barracks, on its way from St. James's Palace to Frogmore, on the morning of January 20th, 1827.

COTHERSTONE.

TOWARDS the close of the year 1827 the boy was
sent to a boarding school, kept by a master
named Smith, at Cotherstone, in the North Riding of
Yorkshire, six miles distant from Barnard Castle.
From his own description of life at this establishment,
written in 1834,* several years before " Nicholas
Nickleby " appeared, it would seem a logical inference
upon a comparison of the two descriptions to say
that this school was the veritable Dotheboys Hall of
Mr. and Mrs. Squeers, so graphically described by
Charles Dickens. As, however, that great author has
expressly stated in his preface of the work that " Mr.
Squeers is representative of a class, not an individual,"
it would be futile to endeavour to establish the identity
of Cotherstone or any other particular school with
" Dotheboys Hall." Such attempts have repeatedly
been made, and have failed, and it seems advisable to
avoid adding one more to the list of failures.

* The written description of the life at this school was given, together
with the Diary in Sweden, to Mrs. Luxmore, at Plymouth, in 1835, and
remained in her possession till 1877. The writer mentions this fact to
prove that it could not by any possibility have been copied from the
picture of " Dotheboys Hall." It has been thought advisable to alter
the order of the narrative, with a view to making it read more consecu-
tively, but no detail is given which does not appear in the original.

But as the description of the life at this School, which now for the first time appears in print, coincides in so many details with the system at " Dotheboys Hall at the delightful village of Dotheboys," it may be interesting to append as footnotes all closely corresponding passages in " Nicholas Nickleby," and so afford a comparison of the two versions, and it is hoped that their consistency will render a mutual service by pointing to the truthfulness of the pictures drawn of a Yorkshire School of the period.

The manuscript runs thus,—

" My father had long been speaking of putting me and my brother to a boarding school, and being taken with Mr. Smith's advertisement in a news paper in which he described himself as ' a benevolent teacher of youth,' called upon him at the Belle Sauvage Inn, Ludgate Hill, whither he used to repair periodically, for the purpose of securing new pupils, and was then staying on one of these ventures.* Not finding him at home he left his card, and on the following day this worthy gentleman entered our house, demonstrated or at least attempted to demonstrate

* " Mr. Squeers is in Town and attends daily from one till four at the Saracen's Head, Snow Hill."

"At Midsummer," muttered Mr Squeers, resuming his complaint, " I took down ten boys."

"Perhaps you recollect me?" said Ralph, looking narrowly at the schoolmaster, "You paid me a small account at each of my half-yearly visits to Town for some years, I think, sir," replied Squeers.

with great warmth the excellency of his system, called
his scholars 'his dear children,'* and, in fact, so won
the respect of my unsuspecting parents that my father
thought him a happy man, and my mother regarded
him as a saint. I was to learn 'good breeding,' and
he engaged to teach me the classics, mathematics, etc.,
with board and lodging also, all for the moderate sum
of £20 per annum.† How well he fulfilled his promise
will be hereafter shown, suffice it to say that parents
cannot be too careful of sending their children to such
places as this turned out to be. If they wish their

---

* "My dear child," said Squeers, "All people have their trials . . .
you are leaving your friends, but you will have a father in me, my dear,
and a mother in Mrs. Squeers."

"My dears, will you speak to your new play-fellow a minute or two."

† "Education at Mr Wackford Squeers' Academy, Dotheboy's Hall,
at the delightful village of Dotheboys, near Greta Bridge, in Yorkshire.
Youth are boarded, clothed, booked, furnished with pocket money,
provided with all necessaries, instructed in all languages, living and
dead, mathematics, orthography, geometry, astronomy, trigonometry,
the use of the globes, algebra, single-stick (if required), writing,
arithmetic, fortification, and every other branch of classical literature.
Terms, twenty guineas per annum. No extras, no vacations, and diet
unparalleled."

(Mr. Snawley), " Twenty pounds per annum I believe Mr. Squeers."
"Guineas" rejoined the schoolmaster with a persuasive smile. "Pounds
for two, I think Mr. Squeers," said Mr. Snawley, solemnly. "I don't
think it could be done, sir," replied Squeers, as if he had never considered the proposition before. "Let me see : four fives is twenty,
double that, and deduct the——, well a pound shall not stand betwixt
us. You must recommend me to your connection, sir, and make it
up that way."

"Now, Nickleby" said Squeers, coming up at the moment buttoning
his great coat, "I think you'd better get up behind. I'm afraid of one
of these boys falling off, and then there's twenty pound a year gone."

sons to be adepts at all kinds of roguery and mischief, and are anxious to see them exalted in this peculiar manner above their fellow men, why then, by all means, send them to one of the cheap Yorkshire boarding schools.

" However, to this fellow's care my brother George and myself* were entrusted, and we made our voyage with him in a brig bound to Stockton-on-Tees, which occupied several days, our fellow passenger, being a cockney girl who was going to Stockton for her health, the captain's wife and children, a monkey, who was a venerable patriarch, and a pig. Mrs. Smith, tender-hearted creature! had driven all the way from the academy (or prison) a distance of thirty-six miles, to meet her beloved husband, and was waiting for us at the inn on arrival, but being, as I said before, a tender-hearted creature, and being moreover afraid that the joy of meeting her husband might prove too much for her weak nerves, she had fortified her courage with a good bolus of brandy, so that when we met her she was in high spirits, and received us with a cackling noise and much glee.†   Smith, in his turn, refreshed

* *Cf.* second quotation in preceding note.

† " They had not been in the apartment a couple of minutes, when a female bounced into the room, and seizing Mr. Squeers by the throat, gave him two loud kisses, one close after the other, like a postman's knock."
" How is my Squeery," said the lady in a playful manner and a very hoarse voice.   " Quite well, my love," replied Squeers.

himself and prepared to depart. It was already dark, and I remember the wind howled fearfully, but he was determined to go in spite of everything, and even the remonstrances of his wife could not move him, and away we rattled. It was very dark, but the horse was perfectly acquainted with the road—I say the horse, because my master was so drunk that he could scarcely keep his seat.* As far as my brother and myself were concerned we were snugly stowed away in a corner of the nondescript vehicle† in which we rode, although both of us felt lost in fear and grief. We jogged along as well as the rough road would permit, my mistress, who was sitting beside me, having had frequent recourses to the bottle, at last fell asleep, and

---

* " Mr. Squeers got down at almost every stage to stretch his legs, as he said, and as he always came back from such excursions with a very red nose and composed himself to sleep directly, there is reason to suppose that he derived great benefit from the process."

" Mr. Squeers treated himself to a stiff tumbler of brandy and water, made on the liberal half-and-half principle, allowing for the dissolution of the sugar, and his amiable helpmate mixed Nicholas the ghost of a small sample of the same compound."

† " At the same time there came out of the yard (*i e.* yard of the George and New Greta Bridge] a rusty pony chaise and a cart, driven by two labouring men. " Put the boys and the boxes into the cart " said Squeers, rubbing his hands, " and the young man and I will go on in the chaise."

" Is it much further to Dotheboy's Hall, sir ?" asked Nicholas. "About three miles from here," replied Squeers, " but you need'nt call it a Hall down here, the fact is it ain't a Hall," observed Squeers, drily. Compare also the postscript to Newman Noggs' letter to Nickleby. " If you should go near Barnard Castle there is good ale at the King's Head."

so continued until we arrived at the first turnpike gate. The custodian was asleep in bed, and did not stir until my master had called him several times, cursed him as many, and flung handfuls of beans, which he had in his overcoat pocket, at his window. When he did arouse the sleeper, he too, took a similar view of the interruption, sending to the d——l all coaches, horses, gigs, and vehicles whatsoever."

After a tedious drive they reached Cotherstone, on the borders of the North Riding of Yorkshire, a few miles from Barnard Castle, and the narrative continues :—

" There were about fifty boys. The building had formerly been a nunnery, and was built in the form of a square, with a courtyard in the centre, into which all the windows looked, the exterior presenting dead walls. There were two gates at opposite sides of the square, which were locked every night at eight o'clock, thus debarring all exit.* On one side of the square was a playground, out of which we were not allowed to go more than once or twice a month, and into which we were turned on the morning after our arrival. Never shall I forget the heart-sinking I felt at the

* " While the schoolmaster was uttering these and other impatient cries, Nicholas had time to observe that the school was a long, cold looking house, one storey high, with a few straggling out-buildings behind, and a barn and stable adjoining. After the lapse of a minute or two the noise of somebody unlocking the yard gate was heard, and presently a little lean boy, with a lantern in his hand issued forth."

C

sight of the crowd of unhealthy young ragamuffins, with their hardened faces, who surrounded us and treated us to jeers and laughter. Other realities of our situation were soon apparent : our clothes were taken from us, only to be returned on occasional Sundays when we attended church at the neighbouring village of Romaldkirk, and others of a workhouse quality substituted, while our shoes were replaced by wooden clogs.* Our bed-rooms, three in number, were little better than granaries. In each room were fourteen or fifteen wooden beds with straw mattresses, and each with a couple of blankets.† Our dining-room was a large gloomy apartment with an earthen floor,

---

* " But the pupils—the young nobleman ! How the last faint traces of hope, the remotest glimmering of any good to be derived from his efforts in this den, faded from the mind of Nicholas as he looked in dismay around !

" Pale and haggard faces, lank and bony figures, children with the countenances of old men, deformities with irons upon their limbs, boys of stunted growth, and others whose long meagre legs would hardly bear their stooping bodies, all crowded on the view together. . . . There were little faces which should have been handsome, darkened with the scowl of sullen, dogged suffering ; there was childhood with the light of its eye quenched, its beauty gone, and its helplessness alone remaining ; there were vicious faced boys, brooding, with leaden eyes, like malefactors in a jail," etc.

† " Supper being over, and removed by a small servant-girl with a hanging eye, Mrs. Squeers retired to lock it up, and also to take into safe custody the clothes of the five boys who had just arrived.

" In another corner, huddled together for companionship, were the little boys who had arrived on the preceding night, three of them in very large leather breeches, and two in old trousers, a something tighter fit than drawers are usually worn ; at no great distance from these was seated the juvenile son and heir of Mr. Squeers—a striking likeness of

the only articles of furniture being long wooden
benches, at which we stood and ate our miserable
rations—yes, stood, for we had not even chairs. The
schoolroom* was a lofty chamber which I suppose had
been the chapel. It had only one small stove† and our
suffering from cold in the winter was horrible. There
were several large holes in the roof which let in water
in rainy weather. We had two ruffians, who were
styled teachers, beside our master, who seldom, or
never entered the schoolroom but to assist at punishing
the boys, which seemed to give him a hellish delight,
like that with which the ministers of the Holy

his father—kicking with great vigour under the hands of Smike, who
was fitting upon him a pair of new boots that bore a most striking
resemblance to those which the least of the little boys had worn on the
journey down—as the little boy himself seemed to think, for he was
regarding the appropriation with a look of most rueful amazement."

"At length Mr. Squeers yawned fearfully, and opined that it was
high time to go to bed: upon which signal, Mrs Squeers and the girl
dragged in a small straw mattress and a couple of blankets, and arranged
them into a couch for Nicholas."

* "'There,' said the schoolmaster, as they stepped in together, 'this
is our shop, Nickleby.'

"It was such a crowded scene, and there were so many objects to
attract attention, that at first Nicholas stared about him really without
seeing anything at all. By degrees, however, the place resolved itself
into a bare and dirty room, with a couple of windows, whereof a tenth
part might be glass, the remainder being stopped up with old copy-books
and paper. There were a couple of long, old ricketty desks, cut and
notched, and inked, and damaged in every possible way.

"The ceiling was supported like that of a barn by cross beams and
rafters, and the walls were so stained and discoloured that it was impossible to tell whether they had ever been touched with paint or whitewash."

† "There was a small stove at that corner of the room which was
nearest to the master's desk."

Inquisition witnessed the tortures of their victims.
We rose at five, and at eight were assembled in the
dining chamber to breakfast. This consisted of black
bread, milk, and water, and when finished, we repaired to the play-ground, and school commenced at
nine. At one, we again assembled to dine. This meal
was varied every day; milk and bread, then soup, a
small tureen* of it among twelve boys, with about an
ounce of meat to each, often in a putrid state.† None
of the teachers dined with us, they merely superintended the distribution of our often disgusting rations,
like huntsmen feeding a kennel of hounds, which is no
bad resemblance to our dinner parties. At five we
supped off black bread and milk, played till seven, and
were then sent off to bed."

Another regulation of this establishment was that no

---

* " Mrs. Squeers having called up a little boy with a curly head, and
wiped her hands upon it, hurried out of the house into a species of wash-
house, where there was a small fire and a large kettle, together with a
number of little wooden bowls which were arranged upon a board.
Into these bowls Mrs. Squeers, assisted by the hungry servant, poured a
brown composition which looked like diluted pin cushions without the
covers, and was called porridge."

† " ' Uncommon juicy steak, that,' said Squeers, as he laid down his
knife and fork, after plying it in silence for some time.

" ' It's prime meat,' rejoined his lady. ' I bought a good large piece
of it myself on purpose for——'

" ' For what ? ' exclaimed Squeers, testily. ' Not for the——'

" ' No, no; not for them,' rejoined Mrs. Squeers; ' on purpose for
you against you came home. Lor ! you didn't think I could have made
such a mistake as that.'

" ' Upon my word, my dear, I didn't know what you were going to
say,' said Squeers, who had turned pale.

holidays were allowed,* and fond parents as a consolation used to send from time to time hampers containing
among other goods, biscuits and sweetmeats, which
upon delivery were forthwith appropriated by the
stronger young ruffians in the school.

Following the description of school life he proceeds
to describe the effect of the ill-treatment.

" I shall now show the horrible effects, physically
and morally, which hard treatment and bad living
produced on us miserable scholars, many of us sons of
respectable parents, whose hearts would have bled with
anguish had they but known the situation of their
children, in the cruel selfishness which takes possession
of the human heart to the exclusion of all feelings of
humanity—even so it was with us, young as most of us
were. The elder and stronger boys tyrannized in a
brutal manner over the younger and weaker.

" 'You needn't make yourself uncomfortable,' remarked his wife,
laughing heartily. 'To think I should be such a noddy ! Well !'
" This part of the conversation was rather unintelligible, but popular
rumour in the neighbourhood asserted that Mr. Squeers, being amiably
opposed to cruelty to animals, not unfrequently purchased for boy consumption the bodies of horned cattle who had died a natural death :
possibly he was apprehensive of having unintentionally devoured some
choice morsel intended for the young gentlemen."

* " (Mr. Snawley) 'This has made me anxious to put them to some
school a good distance off, where there are no holidays - none of those
ill-judged comings home twice a year that unsettle children's minds so—
and where they may rough it a little, you comprehend.'
" 'The payments regular, and no questions asked,' said Squeers,
nodding his head."

"As their own portions of food were too small to satisfy the cravings of hunger they compelled their younger fellows to hide a part of their scanty fare for their benefit. It was of no use that the little fellow pleaded hunger, and with tears in his eyes, begged of him to allow him to eat: his hard-hearted companion turned a deaf ear to his entreaties and with blows and menaces compelled him to obey.

Finally, he sums up this "master's" method of education as being based on the following lines, the term "principles" being obviously inapplicable.

"1.   To establish a boarding school in some remote corner and out of the reach of human eye.

"2.   To advertize in the newspapers and to procure certain persons as referees.*

"3.   To see that his scholars ere he took them should be provided with a good stock of clothing,† etc.

"4.   When he had got them firmly secured, to take

---

* "'Then as we understand each other,' said Squeers, 'will you allow me to ask you whether you consider me a highly virtuous, exemplary, and well-conducted man in private life, and whether as a person whose business it is to take charge of youth, you place the strongest confidence in my unimpeachable integrity, liberality, religious principles, and ability?' 'Certainly I do,' replied the father-in-law, reciprocating the schoolmaster's grin.

"'Perhaps you won't object to say that if I make you a reference.'

"'Not the least in the world.'

"'That's your sort!' said Squeers, taking up a pen; 'this is doing business, and that's what I like'"

† "Each boy is required to bring two suits of clothes, six shirts, six

away from them their fine clothes, etc., and substitute in their place corderoy, and feed them on the coarsest and cheapest food, add plenty of extras to the quarterly accounts, etc., so as to secure to himself plenty of profit.

"Such was the vagabond that called himself a Teacher of Youth, and to whose ' fatherly care ' (as he expressed it) we were entrusted."

After an incarceration of two years in this youthful prison, an uncle, the Rev. John Abernethy, of Bolton, near Haddington, being in the neighbourhood of the School, bethought himself of paying a visit to his unfortunate nephews, and realizing the ill-treatment to which they had been so long subjected, immediately took them away with him to their indescribable delight.

Forty-seven years after this happy release, in 1876, my father revisited and made some sketches of the scene of his youthful misery which are now reproduced, and to an old villager who had watched him while thus occupied with much interest, explained how he had once been a schoolboy within its dilapidated walls.

pairs of stockings, two nightcaps, two pocket handkerchiefs, two pairs of shoes, two hats and a razor."

"Now the fact was that both Mr. and Mrs. Squeers viewed the boys in the light of their proper and natural enemies ; or in other words, they held and considered that their business and profession was to get as much from every boy as could by possibility be screwed out of him.   On this point they were agreed, and behaved in unison accordingly."

"A good many," the latter remarked, "have been
there at different times, but you are the first as I know
of as has come back to look at the place." He noticed
scrawled on the plaster walls of the dormitory names
which he took to be those of subsequent prisoners,
but none of them of boys he could recall to remembrance.

In the year of the visit to Cotherstone he was one of the
Vice-Presidents of the Institution, and his appreciation
of a timely deliverance from its precincts may be best
conveyed by giving his own words contained in a letter
to his wife, in which, after describing his visit, he wrote,
"I uncovered my head and returned grateful thanks
to the Almighty for guiding me after all to a high
position in my profession, and for giving me a happy
cheerful home."

HADDINGTON.

The next attempt in the selection of a school was
more fortunate, and at the instigation of the uncle
who had so opportunely come to the rescue, and
accompanied by him, he left London in a brig named
Trusty, bound for Leith, with a somewhat medley

To face page 24.

SCHOOL HOUSE, COTHERSTONE.

assortment of passengers, as on his previous sea
passage to Stockton ; the list comprised some quakers
returning to Edinburgh, a clown, harlequin, columbine,
and several half-pay officers, who were largely induced
to patronise these boats by the prospect of securing
several days' rations and billet, possibly if the wind
was unfavourable—to the extent of a week or ten
days—for the very moderate sum of £2. This
particular voyage was a stormy one, and involved
anchoring in Bridlington Bay for some two days,
much to the mental disturbance of the poor panto-
mimists, who were engaged to appear on a certain
night at Edinburgh. The minister too became anxious
at the thought of an empty pulpit at Haddington on
the rapidly approaching Sabbath, and, accordingly,
obtained the captain's consent upon reaching Dunbar
to land; the players also gladly seizing this opportunity
of terminating their sea passage and making their way
to Edinburgh by road. For two years the nephew
attended the Haddington Grammar School, frequently
visiting his uncle at the manse, at the end of which
time, as he had evinced no disposition to become
a minister, he was allowed to follow up his own
inclination to enter upon apprenticeship as a civil
engineer, and placed himself as a pupil to his father,
who was then acting as resident engineer on the
London Dock Works, a situation to which he had

been appointed through the recommendation of Mr.
Telford, the first President of the Institution of Civil
Engineers, and in the capacity of resident, was
answerable in turn to Mr. Henry Palmer, the
engineer in chief.

EARLY EXPERIENCE AS AN ENGINEER.

LONDON DOCKS.

THE resident's office, where he obtained his first knowledge of civil engineering in a practical form, was situated in a narrow lane adjoining Ratcliffe Highway, in the parish of Wapping, where the new apprentice found as junior members of the engineering staff, Messrs. George Parker Bidder, the celebrated calculating boy, father of the late eminent Parliamentary Counsel of the same name, Wickstead, afterwards a well-known waterworks engineer, Peter Barlow, and for a short time his brother William, subsequently engineer for the Tay Bridge, sons of the late Astronomer Royal, all of whom attained positions of eminence in the engineering profession, several reaching the Presidency. The home during this period was in Hermitage Street, Wapping, near "Wapping Old Stairs" and "Execution Dock," and he used to recount his remembrance of seeing a surging crowd on the foreshore of the river between high and low water mark, with the ghastly figures of two unfortunate sailors who had mutinied at sea, and so come under the category of "pirates," suspended in their midst. To this scene his father, George Abernethy, who held some honorary parish appointment, had been summoned on the coroner's jury, and had, with great reluctance, finally decided to comply.

An entry in his diary, September 8th, 1831, briefly records an amusing incident, the scene being Charing Cross, and the occasion, King William the Fourth's Coronation Procession. The entry reads :

" Went to see the Coronation, climbed up on the roof of a house, squall with a butcher. Returned home at eight o'clock." The particulars of this squall were these,—Some buildings near the old Golden Cross Inn were being demolished in order to clear the space now occupied by a portion of Trafalgar Square, and noticing some lads climbing a piece of projecting brickwork at the end of a wall of one of the partly pulled down houses on to the adjoining slate roof, he followed their example, and succeeded in perching among them. Suddenly through a trap door in the roof appeared a burly fellow in a butcher's blouse with a stick in his hand, who summarily ordered all and sundry to quit, and as compliance with the order was somewhat slow, he climbed on to

the roof, and selecting a negro as the most suitable
individual for chastisement, pulled him down by the
legs, and commenced striking him with the stick.
But he had happened on the wrong man. Sambo
assumed a scientific pugilistic attitude, and struck
his assailant many awkward blows, whereupon the
latter called out for help, and a general scrimmage
ensued, which reached its climax when the entire
struggling company disappeared through the floor,
amid a cloud of dust into the room below. My
father managed to escape unhurt, and watched from
a safe distance the guardians of the peace marching
off a selection of the party to limbo, Sambo included,
who looked eminently pleased with himself. A few
moments later the Royal Procession came along and
vociferous cheers were raised for His Majesty as he
passed.

Sights of a very different and debasing character
offered at that time to the public at the Old Bailey,
where executions took place in front of the 'Debtors'
Door' of Newgate prison, and which induced grown-up
citizens, who lacked better judgment to repair to such
scenes of morbid excitement and take their youthful
friends with them, did not fail to leave their ghastly
impressions on his mind.

HERNE BAY.

WITHIN the short space of twelve months, however, after entering upon the apprenticeship,
the London Docks were finished, and George Abernethy
and his son then undertook the construction of a pier at
Herne Bay, a company having been formed in London
to supply the necessary capital, but the duties there as
far as the son was concerned were (on his own admission)
light, and the scene of the few incidents which he could
recall during a year of residence at the then small fishing
hamlet, centre principally around Reculvers and the adjoining marshes, where with a single barrelled flint-lock
gun, he used to spend a large portion of his time in
shooting, repairing for refreshment to the small inn
close by the ruins of St. Mary's Church, kept by a
landlady named Mary Brown, or "Molly Brown," as
she was known to her neighbours. He frequently in
later life made reference to this woman, his recollection

of her having been rendered the more indelible by what
for some time seemed to him to be an unaccountable
trait in the character of an innkeeper—namely, a
distinct refusal to accept any money in payment for
what he had ordered. After this eccentric behaviour
had been displayed as he thought for a sufficiently long
period, he enquired of her the reason for not accepting
any money, and her reply was equally well remembered,
" You're just the very image of my only son who was
drowned at sea, and it's quite enough for me to look at
your face."

Molly had won popularity in the neighbourhood by her
accomplishment as a smuggler, the secret of a successful career in this "nefarious practice," up to that
date, lying in the accurate timing of her transactions
together with a coolness in seeing them through, and
an equal capacity for correctly forestalling other
people's movements at any given time. One winter
evening, at about eight o'clock, she tapped at the
window of his lodgings at Herne Bay, and upon
his opening the door she deposited in the passage a large
untidy bundle, suspended on her back, calculated to
pass as "washing," but inside was a neat little keg of
brandy which she begged him to receive as a Christmas present, and as soon as it was accepted, she
hoisted the remains of " the washing " over her shoulder
and disappeared in the direction of the Reculvers, some

four miles distant, as composedly as she had arrived. Frequently during the later period of his life he expressed an intention of "going over to the Reculvers some day" with the object of ascertaining whether she was still alive, but put off his visit till 1875, which proved to be too late, for a tombstone in Herne Churchyard records the fact of her interment beneath it in 1868.

An acquaintance at Herne Bay at this time following a different vocation in life was a Mr. Charles, proprietor of the solitary windmill, who had lived for a long time in town, and still retained his urbanity of manner, and who never lost an opportunity in conversation of referring to former aristocratic friends, of whom from the frequent mention of his name the Prince Regent was presumably *facile princeps.* On Sundays he would walk to Herne Church dressed in a bright blue surtout with gilt buttons, a buff waistcoat, a shirt with conspicuous frills, knee breeches, black silk stockings, buckles on his shoes, and in his hand a gold-headed cane, which was at intervals tucked under his arm to admit of opening a very neat snuff box. In winter time a radical change of costume was effected, among which the buckled shoes gave place to Wellington boots. He always occupied the same pew—a square, high one—and on a particular Sunday had removed the last named personal incumbrances during service. Towards the close of the sermon he proceeded to re-boot himself, and the tag attached to one of them suddenly failing under the severe test to which it was subjected, his head came into violent contact with his pew, an accident which made it desirable in the interest of all present to close the sermon as expeditiously as possible.

SWEDEN.
1833-34.

IN 1833, while engaged in the building of the pier at Herne Bay, he accepted the invitation of a friend, Mr. Elder, to come and assist in laying out roads to a manganese mine, which that gentleman had recently purchased at Spexeryd, a small village distant some sixteen miles from Jönkoping, in Sweden, and sailed on the 30th of June, in the *Anna Bella*, a Scotch schooner plying between London and Gothenburg, on a voyage to the latter port. This visit to Sweden was, in fact, almost exclusively on pleasure bent and constituted the longest holiday enjoyed during his long busy life, but as it was undertaken on the pretext of laying out roads, and in point of time, comes in the early part of his calling as an engineer, it is here treated in this connection, although entirely *pro formâ*. From a letter, written shortly after arrival to his brother Robert, it is plain that his experience in crossing the North Sea in this craft was far from being an agreeable one. The sea was rough, the cabin accommodation small, and to say the very least of it, unclean. Its unpleasant condition, however, had been fully realized before reaching Gravesend, at which point the schooner anchored for a time, in order to despatch a shore boat to secure some provisions, and a fellow voyager, who shared the same cabin, utilised the opportunity of landing to the extent of procuring some chloride of lime, with which, upon his return, he mixed a certain modicum of water, and freely washed out the cabin berths, greatly to the annoyance of the good captain, and sundry venerable blackbeetles, which had long been quartered there unmolested.

From the date of embarkation he kept a diary of his daily experience as " A stranger in a strange land," and illustrated its pages with various Swedish scenes, several of which will be found reproduced in subsequent pages, and upon his return to England he presented the manuscript to an old lady friend, Mrs. Luxmore, who resided at Plymouth, and who, after a lapse of forty years, returned it through the late Mr. Alexander Lang Elder, of Campden House, Kensington, with the following request :—

" HEADLAND, PLYMOUTH,

" *June 25th*, 1877.

" After my letter was written I was minded of my intention to send through you, if you will kindly take the trouble, to Mr. Abernethy, a journal of a visit to Sweden he made in 1833 and which he presented to me many years ago. Will you say that in preparing for what is sure to happen, I thought it best that the manuscript should be in his own possession, and no doubt in reading it over again his early happy days will recur to him.

"C. LUXMORE."

I will endeavour to give in the present chapter from the journal now before me a description of the voyage to Sweden, and residence there, from the entries contained in its numerous pages, arranging them in a consecutive narrative.

From Gravesend downwards, the river was crowded with shipping, outward bound for various parts of the world, and all slowly and in company, made their way as far as the Nore, at which point they separated from one another, and (to use his own expression), " shot off like the rays of the sun in all directions." "These," he wrote, "are the rays of Britain's star, which, by the agency of these oaken messengers, has spread the light of intelligence over the Earth." . . . " What a restless creature man is: not content with flitting about like a ' Will of the Wisp' himself, he causes a sober stately oak, which has stood in the selfsame spot, fanned by the breezes of a hundred summers, to dash over the ocean, and ' Walk the waters like a thing of life.' "

On the morning of the fourth day of the voyage the *Anna Bella* hove in sight of the Naze of Norway, and approaching the coast of Jutland at the Skaw, she thence

Elsborg Castle.

H. 1893.

To face page 36.

stood over towards Sweden, reaching Marstrand late on the 25th, and at daybreak on the 26th dropped anchor off the Castle of Elfsborg, where she was duly searched, and her bill of health examined, before being permitted to proceed up the River Gotha to Gothenburg.

The wind having fallen to a calm and there being, consequently but little prospect of the schooner reaching her destination that day, he engaged a small rowing boat, and proceeded up the river, passing en route the Government Dockyards, in which lay a number of schooner-rigged gunboats, well adapted by their light draught for the difficult navigation of the Baltic. A little nearer the town were the merchant ships of various nations, among which the American flag seemed at that time to predominate.

Upon reaching the suburb of Klippa, he landed, and after reporting his arrival at the Custom House, proceeded on foot to Gothenburg by a fine broad road, planted on either side with trees, and frequented by the elite of the town in summer as a fashionable promenade. His steps as a traveller were naturally directed in search of an hotel, and, upon enquiry, he was directed to a large, shabby looking building of coarse red brickwork, over the doorway of which, on a small wooden tablet about one foot square, was painted " Tod's Hotel."

A Swedish girl opened the door, and conducted him into a clean and comfortable room, in which, upon the floor, in place of a carpet, were strewn small branches of spruce, a supply of which was kept in a box in the corner of the room. Instead of a fireplace there was a glazed earthenware stove, the bottom of which contained burning wood, the smoke ascending the hollow stove and thence passing into the chimney. When the wood has been reduced to glowing embers a flue at the top is closed, and the heat thus retained in the stove.

The fair conductor, however, was almost wholly unacquainted with the English language, and the guest being no better qualified for opening any conversation in her mother tongue, all attempts to represent the fact that he wanted breakfast and lodging for a few days seemed destined to be futile.

At this juncture, however, the guest apparently to some extent lost his temper, in so far that he was heard to mutter d-m-n. "Eh Englesman," said the damsel, smiling, and disappearing for a few moments, returned, bringing with her the landlord, one George Tod, who, it subsequently transpired, had emigrated from Fifeshire, some twenty years before, and upon the advent of this personage, materials for a hearty breakfast were soon forthcoming. The meal being ended and a bedroom duly allotted to him, the newly arrived " Englesman " walked along the main street until he reached a high

GOTHENBURG.

To face page 39.

rock, upon which he climbed, and from its summit obtained a bird's-eye view of the town, which enabled him to write the following description of Gothenburg:—

"Immediately beneath me was the main street, intersected by a wide canal, which is crossed at intervals by draw-bridges, and dotted with numerous boats. Several other streets are intersected by a canal, and some of them bordered with trees. The town has not a very imposing appearance, being built on a plain, and the only prominent edifices are its two churches on the outskirts. The streets are quite straight, and generally cross each other at right angles; they are wide and clean, but badly paved, and there are no causeways for foot passengers. The Gotha meanders in an easterly direction until it vanishes among the distant hills: westward lies the crowd of shipping: while on the north and south are high precipitous rocks, studded with trees and houses. The distant rocky hills are but scantily clothed with pines, among which, here and there, peep the country seats of the merchants. The town is built for the most part along the river, and is nearly surrounded by rocks." A closer inspection of the town, subsequently, enabled him to give a more detailed description. "The shops are scarcely to be distinguished from private houses, except for the fact of the former having a small wooden board

over the door, on which is painted the name of the
occupant, together with a sign illustrative of the craft
pursued within. Thus, tailors exhibit a small pair
of scissors. They are all independent fellows, and
seem to regard their customers as the parties obliged
by any transaction.

"The town is lighted by oil lamps, which are suspended from an iron chain stretched across the street,
one end being made fast to the wall, and the other
passed through a pulley, and thence downwards to a
wooden box placed at a convenient height where it
is secured by a pin.

"About half-way along the main street is a large
square, in which are situated the handsome Town Hall
and the Market Place. In this space were drawn up
a regiment of horse artillery, a fine body of men, but
their movements struck me as being slow compared
with those of the English.

"The Swedish artillery is reported to be excellent, as
they bestow great attention upon it; but I should suppose it is not quite as they rather confidently affirm,
'the best in the world.' "

While residing a few days in Gothenburg he was a
guest at a certain dinner party given by Mr. Caralin,
an eminent chemist, who lived some two miles out of
the town, at a house called, in English interpretation,
'Jacob's Hall,' and in a letter of July 12th, 1833,

addressed to his parents at Herne Bay, he gave this detailed account of the hospitality he received,—

"Accompanied by my host, we walked up a broad gravel path which led to the mansion. A numerous company were assembled at the door, to all of whom we (*i.e.*, Mr. Elder and himself) were introduced: first, to a little jolly-looking fellow, in a blue surtout, and Hessian boots, and wearing a gold watch-chain on which hung a cross, and a silver star on his breast. This was the bishop of the district. Among the rest was Baron Berzelius, the celebrated scientific chemist. Several of the gentlemen wore orders. Upon entering the house, we were ushered into the drawing-room, where we found the table laid out with schnaps, bread, butter, and cheese, and each of the company took a morsel, and a glass of liqueur. We then entered the dining-room, and while grace was being said each person stood behind his chair; after which, all bowed to the host, and then to the ladies, and these preliminaries over, seated themselves and prepared for action.

"The dinner, of about a dozen courses, was excellent. The meats were carved by the servants, and the guests handed the plates from one to another—a decided improvement on the old English system. I must confess I ate a great deal too much, for I had a complaisant Frenchman for a neighbour, who would have me eat of every dish that came round, but still I cut but a poor figure beside the rest of the company. Some of the dishes were nauseous to my palate — raw salmon, beef swimming in oil, etc. All the wine was consumed during dinner, towards the end of which a large bowl was introduced, into which some bottles of claret was poured, together with a quantity of sugar, and some bitter oranges. This was emptied to the health of all present. Mr. Caralin proposed the health of the Englishmen at the table—four in number—in reply to which, at a signal from our host, all rose, bowed to each other, and, after a concluding grace had been said, dispersed. The gentlemen then conducted the ladies to the drawing-room, after doing which they went into the garden, or to the smoking-room, each being at liberty to do as best pleased him. Coffee, tea, ices, etc., were handed round by the servants to the scattered company. For my part, I walked to a small summer-house which commanded an extensive view of the town of Gothenburg, and made a sketch of it. About 9 p.m., all again entered the house to sup, after which the guests took leave. I regretted, exceedingly that I did not understand the Swedish language, as I lost all the conversation which was going on between Berzelius and others of the company."

But festivities at Gothenburg were only of short duration, for on July 4th, the journey to Jönköping, which was distant 112 English miles, had to be

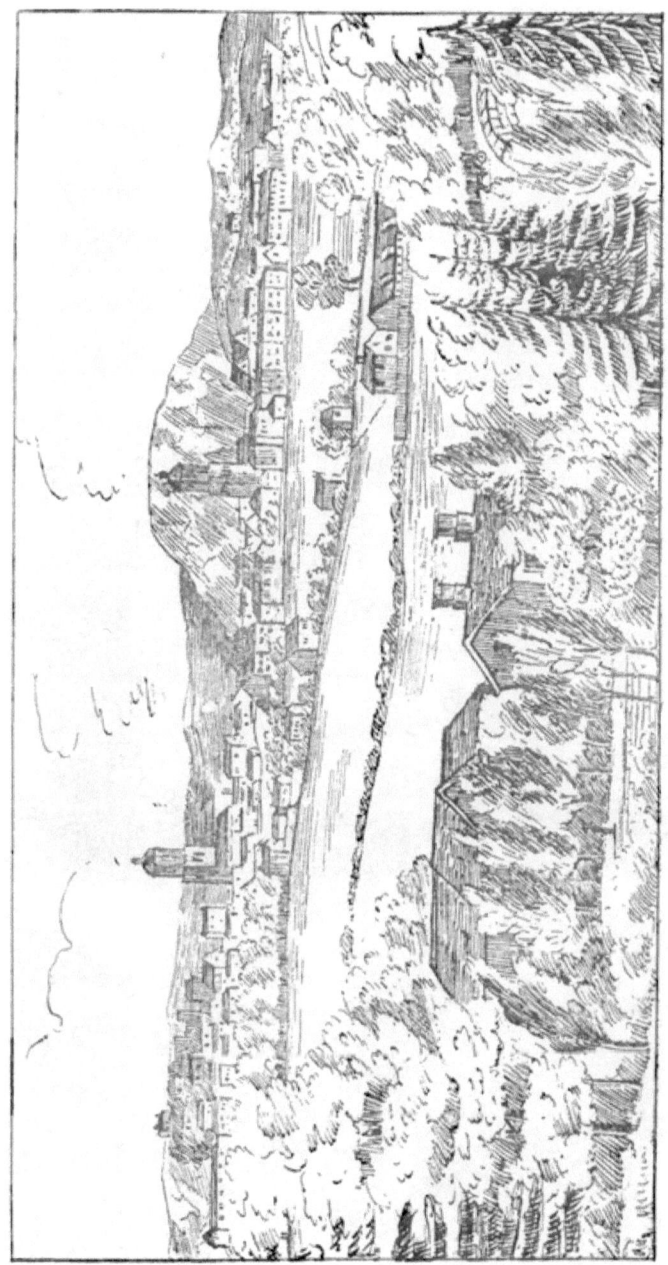

GOTHENBURG, FROM MR. CARALIN'S GARDEN.

To face page 42.

undertaken in order to reach the manganese mine at
Spexeryd, a small village some 15 miles beyond that
town. Accordingly, having secured a "jagtvan," a
vehicle like a small waggon, and in size not much
larger than those drawn by dogs through the London
streets at that date, fitted with a cross seat suspended
at either end by leather straps which somewhat lessened
the jolting over the numerous loose stones, the journey
was commenced about noon. Having proceeded about
eight miles from the town, the travellers came to a
narrow ravine, at the foot of which ran a stream ; on
the bank adjoining some large cotton mills were at
the time in course of construction. Following the
road, which in its turn followed the line of the bank,
the vehicle at length turned a sharp angle in the road
and a large lake came into view, its bright waters
contrasting prettily with the sombre pines which
skirted the margin. Continuing the journey through a
pine wood the road emerged close to another lake
adorned with little islands. On the summit of the
rock, which rose abruptly from this lake, was a chateau,
with a red painted roof, steeply pitched to guard against
the lodgment of snow in the winter, while several
picturesque smaller buildings were discernible among
the pines. A little later the first post-house was
reached and a considerable time occupied in finding and
catching the horses which were required to relieve

the tired ones. At last the route was continued through
an undulating country, the natural features of which
were a series of lakes, pine forests, and rock, until the
small town of Alingsas was reached, and quarters
obtained for the night.

An early start was effected the following morning
and they proceeded on their journey through country
of a different nature. The grand scenery which
accompanied the previous day's travel was changed
to wild barren moorland, with huge boulders of
rock strewed over its surface, and broken only occasionally by the glimpse of a small cultivated patch,
and a miserable wooden cabin appendant to it,
illustrative of the extreme poverty of the peasantry in
the district. At mid-day, the "jagtvan" entered an
extensive forest of birch trees, through which they
travelled for some hours, but upon approaching Jönkoping these were again replaced by a series of pine
forests. The pines, which had grown very straight,
and to a great height, were evidently very old. Some
of them had their lowest boughs at least twenty feet
from the ground. Not a single soul, nor a habitation
were seen for hours, and a solemn silence reigned
supreme until Jönkoping was reached towards midnight, but the halt there was of brief duration, and a
fresh relay of horses being procured, the travellers
pressed on towards the village of Spexeryd, a distance

of fifteen miles, through a continuation of the gloomy pine forests. When six miles distant from Spexeryd, the road became so rough that it was almost impossible to proceed in the darkness which had set in, and the driver, Schuss Bonde, declined to follow the path further until daylight. Thereupon, the travellers alighted and continued on foot by a narrow track, of which they eventually lost all trace, and found themselves in a bog, sinking over their knees. Having extricated themselves from this, they wisely determined to remain where they were till daylight; for a few hours they were subjected to a weird experience listening to the wind sighing through the dark funereal pines overhead, while a great horned owl was occasionally heard uttering his melancholy cry. At length daylight broke and they were enabled to regain the "jagtvan" and to reach the cottage at Spexeryd, where they were received with a hearty welcome from the two Englishmen already quartered there. One of these was Mr. Alexander, a mechanical engineer, who had erected an unworkable water-mill for Mr. Elder, and the other "a young scapegoat, who had been invited over from England, to keep him out of mischief at home, but who managed to get into the same even in this out of the way spot, whenever any slight opportunity offered itself."

The cottage at Spexeryd was situated on a terrace,

near the brow of a hill. Immediately in front rose
a rock to a height of about forty feet, beautifully draped
with velvet moss, and graced with several elegant
specimens of the weeping birch, while above the rock
serving as a background was the outskirt of a large pine
wood. At the back of the cottage the ground fell
abruptly, and the road by which it was approached,
wound in a spiral manner to the foot of the hill, where
it crossed over a brook by a rustic bridge. Cockspur
and wild geranium were the two principal flowers of
the hillside, and of forest trees, the spruce, Scotch fir,
birch, aspen, and hazel were all to be seen mingling
their foliage in charming variety.

The duties in superintending the making of roads
were somewhat intermittent and not of an arduous
nature, and a good deal of time during the day, as well
as in the evenings, was passed in making experiments
with manganese, with the aid of a chemical handbook,
in a workshop adjoining the cottage. One successful
result was a powder, which served as a pigment for
sketching, and which the accompanying illustration of
the little church close by, and others which will be
found on subsequent pages, proves to have been of a
permanent quality, for they have faded little, if at all,
during the sixty-three years since the preparation was
used.

The manganese mine in the vicinity of Spexeryd,

SPEXERYD CHURCH.

To face page 46.

To face page 47.   INTERIOR OF THE CHURCH AT SPEXERYD.

which had already been worked to a depth of 100 feet
at the time of making a roadway to join the high road
to Jönkoping, yielded a considerable amount of ore, and
frequent journeys on horseback had to be made to that
town, where there was a wharf for its shipment, viâ
Lake Wenner and the Gotha Canal, to Gothenburg.
For these trips he engaged the services of a black horse,
named "Beelzebub," in consequence of his behaviour
to his former master, who, after many uncomfortable
experiences on his back, had finally been thrown,
with the result that the horse had been pronounced
a vicious beast, and as such sentenced to be shot.
Beelzebub, however, obtained a reprieve upon the offer
of a small Norwegian pony, Leila, in exchange. The
pony was accepted, and Beelzebub handed over with
the parting words, "go and break your necks together then." By a course of kind treatment, however, and ministration of small rye cakes on occasions
of marked improvement in behaviour, Beelzebub soon
became quiet and gentle, neighed upon his new master
entering the stable, and carried him safely for the
remainder of his stay at Spexeryd.

The road by which he used to travel to Jönkoping
entered that town through a large gateway, over which,
inscribed on the frieze, were the words "Carl Johan
rex." The town then consisted of one long street,
which was badly paved, the houses on either side being

built of wood, and painted red. Near the centre stood the wooden theatre and court house, while the last named and the church were the only two stone build-ings in the town. Being the judicial centre of the province of Smaland, a large proportion of the popula-tion of four thousand were lawyers, who wore a uniform of their own.

Frequently it was necessary to stay at Jönkoping for the night, and he has given an account of a stay on one occasion at a "Wärdhus" (hotel), where "in the evening several Swedish gentlemen joined the party and remained till midnight. Instead of singing songs, as is the custom in England, the Swedes, on these occasions, relate anecdotes, and he is regarded as the most agreeable fellow, who possesses the greatest stock. Each displayed great eagerness to deliver his story, and the moment one of them paused in his narrative another filled up the interval with a few words of his own, so that by the time the first speaker had finished, the other had made considerable progress with what he wanted to say." On the following day there was a fair, and the market place was crowded with bonders, or peasants, dressed in very varied, but becoming costumes. Among them were many Dalcartians, whom he thus describes: "The men are dressed in white flannel coats, knee breeches, broad brimmed hats, and a leather belt round their middle, while

VIEW OF JÖNKÖPING.

To face page 48.

the women wear short dresses, red stockings, and high heeled shoes. The Dalcartians seem to be a distinct race, with dark eyes and hair, and to bear about the same relationship to the Swedish peasantry, as our Scotch Highlanders do to the Lowlanders. They are noted for their tenacity in upholding old customs, and the aversion they show to all that is foreign. These people wander southwards in the summer as far as Germany, and engage themselves in making and selling clocks, as well as rings, crosses, and various trinkets of plaited horse hair."

There were also several " Tartars " or gipsies, who appeared to resemble their brethren in England in their appearance and habits.

The bonders for the most part wear coarse blue cloth round hats and silk handkerchiefs round their necks, while the women dress in scarlet jackets, short blue petticoats reaching to the knees, a white handkerchief wrapped loosely round their heads, and the feet are devoid of boots.

Rides from Spexeryd to Jönkoping during the winter months were apparently at times attended by some elements of danger as the following unpleasant experience will show:—Late one evening he noticed some important papers lying on the sitting-room table, accidently left behind by Mr. Elder, who had ridden to Jönkoping in the afternoon, with the intention of

E

remaining there for the night. Knowing that the
particular business could not be transacted until the
papers were to hand, he saddled Beelzebub with all
despatch and started off for the town. The route
from Spexcryd to the high road was by a bridle path
through a pine forest, and while making his way along
the track, the horse suddenly snorted and set off at
full gallop, and all efforts to pull him up were unavail-
ing. In order to avoid being unseated by coming into
contact with the fir boughs which overhung the path,
the rider had to stoop, and hold on to the animal's
neck, and in this manner he was borne through
the pine forest, and for a considerable way
down the high road until he came near to a post-
ing house, where Beelzebub slackened his pace. The
rider dismounted, and once more the animal's life
was in the balance in consequence of his unmanageable
conduct. The posting-house keeper, however, explained
that the master, instead of abusing the animal, should
on the contrary, feel much indebted to his fleetness, as
some wolves had been seen that day in the neighbourhood, and most probably it was they which had scared
and followed in pursuit of Beelzebub. After this
adventure, the horse and his owner became sworn
friends.

Many pleasant days were spent in hunting and shooting in the neighbourhood, and a few anecdotes

VILLAGE OF SPEXERYD

To face page 51.

connected with both, may be of interest to the
reader. Hearing, upon one occasion, of some wolves
having attacked and destroyed a couple of cows on the
previous evening, which were depastured at a short
distance from where he was living—he procured a
portion of one of the carcases, and in the company of
a Swede, carried it next morning to a spot in the forest
supposed to be frequented by wolves. Here he set
to work to build a hut of pine branches, and made
preparations for watching during the coming night.
All being in readiness he went home, and at about
nine o'clock, returned to the appointed station,
armed with a gun and axe, the Swede bringing the
same selection of weapons. He confesses to have
experienced a sensation of ' creepiness ' while stationed
in the gloominess of the pine forest, watching for the
expected visitors. There was very little undergrowth
around, save here and there a juniper bush, but the
ground was covered with moss, and its even surface
broken at intervals with numerous large ant hills. The
night, however, was very dark, and the bait placed on
the trunk of a tree, some twenty yards distant, was
barely visible. The hours passed slowly by, and a deep
silence reigned around the hut, broken only by an
occasional doleful mope of an horned owl, as he flitted
overhead. Neither of the hunters spoke, but crouched,
with their eyes fixed towards the bait. Near midnight,

faint sounds as of an animal panting were detected,
and a few seconds later, a figure, the outline of which
resembled a wolf, was espied some thirty yards distant,
standing quite motionless beside the bait. The Swede
took a long aim and discharged his gun, and a loud cry
followed the report. Both darted through the smoke
with their axes to give the *coup de grace*, but there was no
trace of the animal. A few days after, a farmer complained to him that his large sheep-dog had been
peppered with shot in the hind quarters by some un-
known person, which caused the sportsmen to shrewdly
suspect that it was the farmer's dog they had fired at.

The appearance of wolves in the neighbourhood
had, however, caused sufficient excitement among the
peasantry to induce them to hold a " skall " at the end
of the week, and in the diary of the 12th July an
account is given of the organised wolf hunt. " Yesterday, what is called a ' skall ' took place for destroying
the wolves, at which about two hundred persons were
present. The custom here is, that a person whose
cattle have been injured or killed by wolves, after
having given due notice of the fact to the jagtmästre
(hunting master) of the district, can call upon all males
in the parish over twenty years of age to attend the
meet, each armed with a gun or bludgeon. On this
occasion the company formed themselves into a circle
of about half a mile in diameter, each at a short dis-

SPEXERYD. SWEDEN.

To face page 52.

tance apart. At a given signal from the huntsman, all moved forward in silence, gradually contracting the circle, until it was only some three hundred yards in diameter. Two wolves had been surrounded, but though several shots were fired they broke through the ring. One of them, however, was severely wounded, and could not run very fast. The ' skall ' forthwith broke up, every one starting off in pursuit of the wounded animal, which was soon run down and killed. It was an old male, but being summer time he was of a dirty brown colour."

One more experience with "vargs" is recorded :—

"While walking home I caught sight of a wolf sitting on its haunches in a cleared piece of the wood at a little distance off, intently watching some cattle feeding. They seemed to be fully alive to their danger, for they were standing in line with their heads lowered, when suddenly one of the oxen separated from the rest and made a determined dash at the wolf, who seemed rather intimidated, and inclined to move off. At this moment I discharged the contents of my piece after him, though doubtless it had no other effect than that of accelerating his pace."

Capercaillie (tyedars) were to be found, though not plentifully, in the pine forests in the vicinity of Spexeryd, and the various methods of stalking these

fine birds practised by the Swedes are described.
Sometimes they would take a small dog with them to
detract the birds' attention while they were approached,
and at others place a decoy bird made of cloth on a
tree and imitate the chuckling note of the tyedar,
resembling 'pelr, pelr,' which attracts the hen birds
particularly. A third method is to enter the woods at
night with a torch, again imitating the birds' call, the
torch being employed to interest the bird, and divert
attention from the gunner in the same way as the
small dog in the day time, but in each method the
end for which these means are devised, is the same,
viz., to 'pot' the bird sitting."

Towards the autumn of 1833 he accepted an invitation to stay at the house of a Swedish nobleman
named Captain Quickfeldt, who lived in a château
called Werisjoo, some eight miles from Jönkoping,
and upon the termination of his visit, he wrote a
detailed account of the domestic life there. "The
wooden house has a lofty, red-tiled roof, with numerous
out-buildings of a like description, which are used
as rooms for the servants, and perhaps some guests
if there is a large party, which is often the case in
winter. A cracked bell on a pole, and a walled
garden, complete the establishment. There is no
lawn or gravel paths as in England. These noble-
men keep a good stable of horses, and many servants

who cost but little, and are necessary, for the nobles
farm their own estates, buy and sell cattle, and even
distil whisky to sell. The interior of the house consists of a number of large carpetless rooms, barely
furnished, and the little furniture there is of the
plainest material. One portion is sacred to the ladies,
and the gentlemen seldom enter there. Their apartments are often carpeted and handsomely furnished;
indeed it would not do to carpet the apartments of
the men, as they are all great smokers, and spit about
in every direction."

" We generally rose at seven o'clock and partook of
coffee, after which we read or amused ourselves somehow
till ten, when we breakfasted on beef steak, potatoes,
etc., drinking with them porter or wine. We then
rode or walked till two, and returned and dressed
for dinner, at which meal the ladies made their appearance for the first time. The dinner consisted usually
of a great variety of dishes, but the Swedish cooking
is not at all agreeable to an English palate, the meat
swimming in grease, and the vegetables, such as cabbage
and lettuce, being served up with sugar. The Swedes
are great eaters, and take little exercise, and keep a
high temperature in their rooms by means of their
earthenware stoves. Consequently they have sallow
complexions, and seldom attain a great age.

" After dinner we enjoyed the society of the ladies

playing chess, cards, etc., with music on the harp
and piano ; several of the gentlemen played well on
the flute. The music is slow and pathetic, some of it
exceedingly fine. At ten o'clock we had supper, and
then retired to bed. Occasionly in the winter, especially
on Sundays, the evenings were enlivened by a ball,
which was always a gay sight, owing to the variety
of military and other uniforms worn. In the square
dances, the ladies and gentlemen keep at opposite ends
of the room. The favourite dance is a sort of quadrille,
which they term ' à la Française,' but it is a sorry imita-
tion, and they finish every figure by jumping as high
as they can. The waltzing is still worse : they take
very long steps and spin round the room like two
cockroaches on one pin.

" Most of the nobles keep a 'carrosse,' a heavy
lumbering vehicle, like the old-fashioned London
hackney coach. Their sledges, for winter travelling,
are very handsome. Bells are attached to various parts
of the harness, for as they drive very fast, and in
narrow roads, accidents would often occur were it not
for this precaution."

Another and somewhat more facetious description
is given of the quiet life typical of the Swedish
nobility.

" His château is placed on the most exposed part of

A LAKE NEAR SPEXERYD.

To face page 56.

his estate, so that he can have his cornfield before him ; such a scene being in his estimation far beyond either the picturesque or romantic. He rises about seven, and having dressed, lights his pipe, and smokes with great solemnity till about nine, when he breakfasts. He then again lights his pipe and stalks forth into the open air, where he may be seen puffing out volumes of smoke and gazing intently on the above-mentioned field of corn, his mind occupied in an abstruse calculation as to how much meal the said field will produce when ground, and the number of loaves he will be enabled to make from it. In this manner he amuses himself till the cracked bell of his wooden château tolls for dinner, at which he gorges himself and takes a siesta."

Of the boors or peasantry this additional description, culled from the pages of his diary, may be given :—

" The men are dressed in jackets, knee-breeches and Hessian boots, and broad-brimmed hats: on Sundays and holidays they are all dressed precisely alike, and they then substitute a surtout for the jacket, and each carries a silver-mounted staff in his hand. They wear their hair long and hanging over their shoulders, possibly to keep the snow in winter from going down their necks . . . . They have generally a good house, and are independent fellows, and when sober, quiet and obliging, paying great deference to their superiors, but quite *vice versâ* when drunk, which is too often the case, and is not to be wondered at considering they possess a small still, and are at liberty to distil what quantity of whiskey they please—they are not, however, allowed to sell any.   .   .   .   Their life is very laborious for so barren is the land that, if he (*i.e.* a bonder) possesses an estate of one or two hundred acres, he can do no more than procure a subsistence, for the greater part of the country is pine forest, and the proportion of permanently cleared land, small   .   .   . while in the valleys are bogs, which grow a long coarse grass, affording food for the cattle."

Occasionally, what are termed temporary clearings, are made in the pine forests in Sweden. A certain batch of trees are felled early in the spring and allowed to lie till autumn to dry. Afterwards they are burnt and the charcoal spread for manure. The cleared ground is then sown with rye, after which, it is perhaps, left untouched for years. One day upon returning from a long ride in the woods, he came upon one of these open spaces, in the middle of which were three upright poles, and upon them were suspended the ghastly remains of a young man who had recently been executed there, the head and right hand had been severed and placed on the outside posts, while the body hung on the centre one. ˙

Towards the end of the year 1835, the sojourn in
Sweden came to an end and he was recalled to England, to again assist his father in the construction of
the Start Point Lighthouse, in Devonshire, under
Mr. James Walker, of London. His diary bears record
that he quitted Spexeryd with much regret, for towards
the end there was the following pathetic entry :—" I
shall always look back to the time when I dwelt in the
secluded Scandinavian pine forest with regret, as I
think I shall have few such happy periods of life
between me and the grave."

This suggests the lines of Lord Byron :—

" My pensive memory lingers on
  Those scenes to be enjoy'd no more,
  Those scenes regretted ever :
  The measure of our youth is full,
  Life's evening dream is dark and dull,
  And we may meet, ah ! never."

START POINT.

JAMES ABERNETHY had completed his twenty-first year when he received the letter from his father asking him to return to England and assist in building the Lighthouse at the Start Point. Very soon after arriving at that lonely headland in Devonshire which was to be the scene of operations during the ensuing twelve months, he was despatched to the small island of Herm, situated some two miles from the Port of St. Pierre, in Guernsey, to superintend the quarrying and dressing of the granite, of which material the Lighthouse was to be built. In a letter to his friend, Mr. Luxmore, he refers to his insular position in these terms :—" This little sea-girt isle is about four miles in circumference, and the inhabitants, some three hundred in number, are all connected with the quarries. I am literally the Deputy Governor, for all here are under my control, and no man can leave the island without an order from my superior or myself." The house in which he stayed belonged to a Colonel Lindsey, but apparently he resided there at that time alone, for he continues:—" I have no society, and not even a friend to talk to, and a sense of loneliness comes over me at times, and I feel so dejected that I could almost throw myself into the sea. It is plain I am not in-tended by nature for a Robinson Crusoe."

The short period of residence at the Start, to which he returned when the work of building the lighthouse was in progress, was equally monotonous and uncon-genial to his taste. An active, energetic man by nature he felt he had a poor sphere in which to display his energy and ability. "I have longed for a letter," he wrote to a friend when the lighthouse was but half built, "communicating the agreeable intelligence that you had procured for me another situation, but I know this is no easy matter in these times. I should feel ever grateful to anyone who would put me in the way of escaping from this miserable place. You no doubt think me very impatient to repine in this manner, but really I cannot help it, living the listless life which I do, and surrounded by perhaps the most uneducated people in England."

The way of escape was shortly afterwards opened, by his father recommending him to Mr. George Leather, of Leeds, for the position of resident Engineer, under that gentleman, in the construction of the Docks at Goole,

with the somewhat characteristic rider as to his qualifi-
cation, " I would not recommend him although he is
my own son if I did not think him capable of taking
the situation," but before concluding the allusion to his
residence at the Start, two episodes connected with the
smuggling then practised are worth mentioning.

One morning the coastguard officer, stationed there,
and whom he knew well, called at the farm-house
where he lodged in a great state of excitement, and
stated that he had found the man on duty near the
lighthouse gagged and bound, early that morning, and
minus his pistol and cutlass. The statement of the
last named, when his gag was removed, was to the
effect that he had been suddenly pounced upon during
the night by several men, who had quickly reduced him
to the condition in which he had been discovered, and
he felt sure some of them were men employed in building the lighthouse, as he perceived, during the struggle,
that they smelt of mortar. Subsequent investigation,
however, never led to any more specific identification
than that, but the suspicion ever remained in the
officer's mind that the navvies had done it, as this
second incident will prove.

Through the headland ran a natural tunnel, along
which my father was in the habit of swimming, and on
one occasion in doing so, struck his knees against a
hard object beneath the surface of the water, and, on

feeling with his hand, discovered that he had come in contact with one of a number of kegs. After he had concluded his swim and dressed, he saw a man watching him from the rocks above, and on passing him, the latter said, with a smile, " I know you are a gentleman and will not say anything." " About what," he enquired, " Oh," observed the man, " you did not swim through the tunnel as usual." " No," he replied, " I found obstacles in the way, but it's all right, you may trust me."

On the following night a small packet was left at the farm house, containing a bottle of very fine brandy, and on the next occasion of the officer paying a visit there a glass of it, in the form of hot grog, was offered to him.

" Hulloa ! " he exclaimed, " where did you get this stuff from ? one of your ' mortary' friends I should think," and ended with a hearty laugh.

GOOLE.

THE removal to Goole in 1836, to act as assistant
engineer under Mr. George Leather, marks the
commencement of his experience in the special branch
of civil engineering, viz : The construction of harbours
and docks, in which he was subsequently to hold the
highest position in the profession, and be termed the
father of marine engineering. Some of the more important of his works will be alluded to in the pages
which follow, but it would be tedious reading were an
attempt made to give the engineering details of each of
them respectively. The fact that they all remain in a
satisfactory condition after, in the majority of cases,
many years of trial by wind and wave, speaks sufficiently, perhaps, for the skilfulness of their design,
their practicability of execution, and efficiency when
completed. Towards their ultimate efficiency and
success all who co-operated contributed, but during
progress and until completion he, as engineer, was
individually looked to as the responsible comptroller,
and it would be true to say that in his own conscience

From drawing of [illegible] Home.
[illegible]

RESIDENCE AT NORMANTON.

To face page 65.

he continued to hold himself responsible for their lasting stability throughout his professional career, a retrospect of which, when nearing its close, afforded him the happy consolation that it was unmarred by any failure.

As yet, however, we must regard him as a young assistant engineer, under Mr. George Leather, at Goole, engaged in the construction of the docks at that town, the contractor for the work being Mr. Hugh McIntosh, of Bloomsbury Square, a successful and practical man of business, although at that time totally blind. In spite of this infirmity he was always enabled by putting a series of apt questions to understand the exact condition and progress of the work. Several small accidents, however, occurred to retard operations from time to time, but strangely enough the last of the series, in which the young engineer nearly lost his life, had the effect of accelerating matters by informally opening the lock. This was brought about by the sudden failure of the cofferdam when the lock was all but finished. The timbering had shown some signs of giving way, and while standing one morning on the bottom of the lock inside the cofferdam directing a gang of navvies how to shore up the timbering, it suddenly cracked, and the dam gave way from end to end, filling the lock, and nearly drowning all who were in it.

Upon the completion of the docks at Goole in the following year, he obtained a similar situation on the

F

Aire and Calder Canal Works, between Wakefield and
Methley, and a few months later the North Midland
Railway enlisted his services to assist in the construction of their line of railway between Wakefield and
Leeds. While engaged by this Company he took a
house at Normanton, and in the same year, 1838,
married Ann, the eldest daughter of John Neill, Esq.,
of Wakefield and Leeds, who lived to prove herself one
of the most devoted of wives and one of the best of
mothers through a period of fifty-eight years.

The residence at Normanton was an old manor
house, on the walls of which hung portraits of
numerous former tenants. Several quaint old houses
of a similar description were to be found at the village
of Alltofts, one of which had formerly been the home
of Admiral Frobisher. The admiral's portrait and
sword were still to be seen, but the sons of the widow,
a Mrs. Denison, who lived in the house, had defaced
the former, and converted the blade of the latter into a
weapon bearing some resemblance to a cross bow.
After some eighteen months service in the employ of
the North Midland Railway Company, he applied for
the post of Resident Engineer to the Aberdeen Harbour
Trustees, and having the good fortune to be the successful candidate, returned in 1840 to his native city,
where shortly afterwards he undertook the first of his
more important works as a dock engineer.

NORMANTON CHURCH.

To face page 66.

ABERDEEN.

1840-51.

THE first year's work at Aberdeen was devoted to dredging the harbour, with a view to obtaining an increased ebb and flow of the tide and the outgoing current of the river Dee was trained during the same period by embankments and other works calculated by the creation of additional scour to increase the depth of the entrance channel. The result was so far beneficial that at the end of twelve months the water over the bar had increased from two feet to six feet at low water spring tides, while the navigation had been facilitated by the erection of leading lights to guide vessels between the piers at night. With this improved condition of the tidal harbour the Trustees applied to Parliament for an Act to convert a large portion of it into a dock. A previous Bill to effect a similar object had been thrown out by the Committee on the ground of defective engineering, and the Harbour Trustees now invited competitive designs. A long wrangle ensued over the designs submitted, but eventually those prepared by the resident engineer were accepted, and the Bill to carry them into effect became an Act in 1841. It was strongly opposed however before the Parliamentary Committee, and this necessitated journeys to London in company with the chairman, Provost Blaikie, afterwards Sir Thomas Blaikie, Alexander Hadden, Master of Shore Works, and John Angus, Town Clerk.

Upon the passing of the act, the resident engineer was called upon to furnish the working drawings and specification, but conditionally, that the result of his work was to be submitted to a leading London engineer for criticism and approval. He was allowed, however, to nominate an expert of his own selection and upon making his choice known at a certain meeting of the Trustees one of them exclaimed "Abernethy man, you've put your head into the lion's mouth, he may bite it off." A few days later, accompanied by Provost Blaikie, he repaired to London to undergo the ordeal of having his elaborate work criticised, and called, by appointment, upon the expert, whom he found seated at a table with his secretary, and in front of him a formidable pile of notes. These notes the secretary dealt out one by one, in the form of questions,

and answers were given apparently with satisfaction to all present until it was asked why the lock invert was to be built of brick instead of granite. The expert objected to the work being of brick, and a somewhat animated argument ensued, but failing to substantiate the selection of brickwork as being the better material to employ by his replies, the candidate for honours brought the discussion to a climax by pointing out that his examiner had himself recently, as an engineer, designed and made a lock invert of the same material as that now complained of, and the interview was thereupon postponed abruptly until the following day. Provost Blaikie, however, was well satisfied with the defence of the plans, and on the way to the Old Hummum's Hotel, Covent Garden, where they were staying, said, "Gae awa back to Aberdeen, and tak yer plans wi ye, we'll waste nae mair time havering about them," and he returned the same evening, at the age of twenty-eight, to undertake the construction of the docks at Aberdeen. The contract to execute the works was let to the contractor who had given the lowest tender, with the result that operations were suspended within a year, owing to failure of capital. At this juncture, with the sanction of the Trustees, the engineer took over the works on their behalf, and finished them successfully in 1848, by the autumn of which year the whole of the tidal harbour had been converted into a dock of 37 acres, approached by a lock 250 feet in length, and 60 feet in width, and with 22 feet of water over the sill at high spring tides. Before the dock was quite completed, an intimation was received by the city authorities that Her Majesty the Queen, His Royal Highness the Prince Consort, and the three Royal children, the Princess Royal, Prince of Wales, and Prince Alfred were to visit Aberdeen, in the Royal Yacht, on Thursday, September 7th. There being no harbour master as yet appointed, the superintendence of the arrangements for disembarking fell upon the engineer. This was the occasion of Her Majesty's first visit to Scotland. Not only had no dock master as yet been appointed, but the lock gates had not been tested since their erection, when the date of the projected visit had arrived. The engineer, who had on the morning of September 6th, received a private note from his friend, Captain Washington, R.N., Hydrographer to the Admiralty, containing the postscript—"N.B., Don't let the Queen catch you napping," was at the works at 5 a.m. on the following morning, seeing to the final touches in connection with the triumphal arch which had been erected opposite to the portion of the quay where the Royal party were to land, but as there was no appearance of the Royal Yacht in the distance some time after the tide had begun to ebb, he concluded that

To face page 70. THE QUEEN LANDING AT ABERDEEN, 1848.

it would not be coming till the evening, and by way of
satisfying himself of the efficient working of the lock
gates, played the role of dock-master in passing in
one of the Aberdeen Steam Navigation Company's
steamers, the *Duke of Wellington*, which had been
offered for this purpose and placed at his disposal into
the lock, and he had just got the trial steamer safely
into the lock, which occupied some considerable time,
when he descried the Royal Standard floating at the
mainmast of the *Victoria and Albert* passing between
the pier heads. This arrival at eight o'clock in the
morning was fully twenty-four hours earlier than was
expected, but still the authorities were not caught
napping as happened to their more southern neighbours
in Edinburgh just before. With all expedition the test
steamer was displaced, and the yacht reached the lock
entrance with Lord Adolphus Fitzclarence, the captain,
on the bridge. Her dimensions had previously been
supplied, and the beam across the paddle boxes was
fifty-eight feet, which was but two feet less than the
width of the lock. Some confusion ensued owing to
the rope fenders, which had been lowered over the
vessel's sides to protect the gilt, jamming, and so pre-
venting her entrance into the lock. His lordship
refused to haul them up, but upon the temporarily
appointed dock-master informing him that the tide
was rapidly falling, and that if the yacht did not

pass in quickly, she would ground on the outer sill, and probably break her back, he ordered them to be taken in, and by a turn of her paddles the yacht passed safely in, and was soon moored at the jetty projecting from the quay. A certain area had been railed off and was guarded by the Harbour Trustees' workmen, who were sworn in as special constables, and the engineer as their chief, is represented in the accompanying picture of the disembarkation, with a staff in his right hand. The morning was bright and cheerful and Her Majesty, on landing, was received by the Earl of Aberdeen, the then Lord Provost, George Thompson, and the Members of the Town Council, headed by John Angus, the town clerk.

After three weeks stay, Her Majesty, on the 28th inst., returned to the yacht from Balmoral, which had been purchased from Sir Robert Gordon, with the intention of returning to Leith by sea. The weather, however, was very stormy, an easterly gale blowing and a heavy sea breaking on the bar. On the following morning Lord Alfred Paget, Her Majesty's Equerry in Waiting, was advised by the Harbour Authorities against proceeding to sea that day, and they further suggested that Her Majesty should return by land. His Lordship agreed, and advised Her Majesty of the proposed alteration in the arrangements and the Royal Party decided to return by land, travelling by carriages

to Perth, thence by rail to Crewe, and reaching Buckingham Palace on the morning of Sunday, October 1st.
The dockmaster's part, however, has not yet been
fully described, for escorting the Royal Yacht were the
steam sloop *Virago*, Commander Harris, and the steam
packet *Vivid*, commanded by Captain, afterwards Sir
Luke Smithett. Seeing the latter preparing to depart,
he informed him of the altered arrangement, and upon
receiving a reply to the effect that he had no other
orders than to proceed to Leith and warn the authorities
of her Majesty's approach, he took it upon himself to
delay passing the vessel out of the lock, until Captain
Smithett had received counter orders from Lord
Fitzclarence. Twenty-two years later he met Sir
Luke Smithett at Dover. The latter had quite for-
gotten him until asked if he recollected his visit to
Aberdeen in command of the *Vivid* and being, to his
great indignation, imprisoned for a certain time in
the lock there. " Yes, I do," he replied. "And you
are my old friend Abernethy, the engineer."

Between the years 1840 and 1851, the period of
residence as Engineer to the Aberdeen Harbour Trust,
one million tons of material were removed from the
bed of the harbour by dredging, exclusive of large
quantities of boulder stones laid bare from time to
time by the constantly increasing action of the outgoing current. The result was the entire removal of

the bar, which may be said to have had no existence since 1851, as the bottom of the channel thenceforward formed a plane gradually inclining seaward.

Extensive breakwaters have since been constructed of solid concrete, which effectually protect the entrance from on-shore gales, and enable vessels to safely enter a port formerly one of the most dangerous on the eastern coast.

While acting as engineer to the Harbour Trustees, he also constructed a fishing harbour at Boddam, near Peterhead, for the Prime Minister, the Earl of Aberdeen, on the recommendation of Captain, (afterwards Admiral) Washington, and visited him several times while the works were in progress, at his seat, Haddo House, and also at his villa at Boddam, in company with his lordship's legal adviser, Mr. James Brebner, an advocate of Aberdeen. At the completion of the harbour at Boddam, he had a long interview with his lordship in London at Argyll House, and received a complimentary note a few days later in answer to a request made to his lordship at the interview to prevail upon the Board of Works to give him an audience with regard to certain works at Birkenhead which he kindly obtained for him. He also designed a bridge over the river Ury for his lordship, a letter from whom, addressed to Mr. Brebner acknowledging the receipt of the design contains the following paragraphs :—

HADDO HOUSE,

"*July 27th*, 1850.

"MY DEAR SIR,

"The sketch of the bridge which you sent yesterday seemed to be a very good plan; and if intended for carriages, wonderfully cheap. I cannot help, however, apprehending that there must be some great mistake in this respect, and that the expense of the whole work will be much more considerable than you imagine.

"The ford is really so good, that a bridge for carriages is not much wanted, as it is only impassable in extraordinary floods; but a foot bridge will certainly be a great convenience, and I should have thought might have been constructed at a very trifling expense. . . . .

"I am, my dear Sir,

"Very truly yours,

"J. BREDNER, ESQ."   "ABERDEEN."

In the year 1849, the subject of the utilization of sewage as manure for grass lands was engaging the attention of the Town Council. A well-known agriculturalist in the county, Mr. Smith, of Deanstone, had strongly advocated a particular scheme, but the authorities were dissatisfied with the report which he had furnished to them, and the Harbour Trustees resolved to send their engineer to Holland and France, to investigate the sewage systems of those countries. Accordingly, in company with one of his pupils, Alexander Jardine, afterwards Sir Alexander Jardine, Bart., the son of the celebrated naturalist,

Sir William Jardine, of "Applegarth," he proceeded, armed with letters of introduction from Lord John Hay and others to the continent, and visited Amsterdam, Rotterdam, the Hague, Brussels (where he was conducted over the Field of Waterloo by a Sergeant Cotton, who had been present at the battle), and finally Paris and Versailles. The upshot of the report, however, written up upon his return, was, that no existing system which he had investigated, was satisfactory in the result.

Home life at Aberdeen was as happy as his first important engineering works there, were successful. During the first two years he lived at "Foot Dee," then in King Street, and for the last four at Union Place, and he made, during the ten years residence in the granite city, the acquaintance of many good friends. Among them Dr. Lizars, a Professor of Surgery at Marischal College, and Dr. James Steel, a very able and experienced physician. Another friend was found in Monsieur de Vitry, an old cavalry officer in the French army, who had been obliged to quit his country in Napoleon's reign, and against whom he was never tired of inveighing. Dr. Steel and he had found De Vitry in an abject state of poverty, and engaged him to teach them French, but the tuition time was chiefly occupied in listening to tales of Royalist plots, and in encounters with the foils in which the old French officer was ex-

ceedingly skilful. The poor old gentleman, who used
to spend all his spare cash in purchasing opium, died
in 1850, and Dr. Steel, who had been his chief friend
in his latter days, was chief mourner at his grave.
Captain Krashminicoff, who commanded the Russian
despatch boat *Vladimer* was another intimate friend.
He had commenced the friendship by introducing himself in the engineer's office, with the object of ascertaining who was the proper person in Aberdeen to
execute certain repairs to the engines of his vessel,
and during his detention of three months, while the
engines were being repaired, he and his wife, an
accomplished musician, were constant guests at King
Street. Mr. James Hall, the shipbuilder, and Mr.
John Rennie, the shipowner, were also among his
more intimate friends.

In the summer months the home was at a cottage
still existing near the Bridge of Feuch, and in some
seasons, at Inverurie, on the river Don, where, as well
as on the Ury, good salmon fishing was to be found.
Rival anglers were found in Captain Hawkins, and
an Alister Frazer, of Culduthal, near Inverness, a
fine old highland gentleman, who frequently invited
him to his country seat, but who regarded the angling
achievements of the younger enthusiast as by no
means approaching perfection.

The writer well remembers hearing the following

anecdote of a day's fishing during one of these visits
to Culduthal. The old gentleman was suffering from
an attack of gout, and hobbled down on crutches to
the river side, at the foot of his lawn, to watch his
guest and his own son, who was also named Alister,
fishing. The former succeeded in hooking a salmon,
and after a long struggle had brought his prize within
gaffing distance, when the son, in his excitement,
stumbled and fell into the water, breaking the line in
his fall and releasing the fish. Next moment one of
the crutches, intended for the son's head, whizzed
into the stream, from which it was subsequently
rescued by the keepers.

He sometimes, too, during the last two years
residence at Aberdeen paid visits to Lord Lovat at
"Beaufort," on the River Beauly, the friendship having
developed from being professionally employed by his
lordship, to restore the normal course of the Beauly,
which flowed through his park, and secure its banks
from being breached by heavy floods.

Subjoined is his lordship's original letter, soliciting
his advice with regard to the state of the river:—

" BEAUFORT,
" February 13th, 1849.

" DEAR SIR.

      " The late floods have done my property a great deal
of injury by the river cutting its banks, which are left in a very
dangerous state. I shall be obliged to you if you could come

here to give me your opinion as to the way they should be
secured to prevent further injury. I hope it will be convenient
for you to come very soon:

" I am, yours truly,

" ABERNETHY, Esq.,   " LOVAT."
    Union Place, Aberdeen.

The harbour works at Aberdeen, while in course of
construction, attracted the notice of Captain Vetch,
R.E. and Captain Washington, and in 1844, principally
through the influence of the latter, he was appointed
one of the Surveying Officers under the Preliminary
Enquiries Act, and served in that capacity for a period
of eight years, at the end of which time the Act was
repealed. During those eight years, however, he inspected and reported upon many schemes for the
improvement of ports and navigable rivers in the
United Kingdom. Chief among the ports inspected
were Liverpool, Birkenhead, Glasgow, Bristol, Newcastle and Belfast, and among rivers, the Tyne, Clyde,
and Ribble. His duties brought him into contact with
many well known engineers, contractors and counsel,
and he acquired considerable experience in listening to
the examination of witnesses by some of the last
named gentlemen.

One of these enquiries held in the Court House at
Coleraine, in April, 1858, relative to certain railway
bridges to be erected over the river Bann, appears to

have been productive of no little amusement. The promoters were represented by a solicitor, Mr. T——, and the opponents of the project also by a solicitor, Mr. K——, and a well known contractor in those days, Mr. D——.

On the first day of the hearing the promoters had put forward a strong case, and were so elated with their success, and the position they had won, or rather thought they had won, by the evidence submitted at the close of the first day's hearing, and which had been unimpaired by cross-examination, that the whole party spent the greater part of the night at Ballymena over a luxurious dinner. But sorrow came in the morning, for Mr. T——'s papers, with which he was to follow up and clinch the victory of the previous day, were all jumbled in hopeless confusion in a carpet bag.

Mr. T——'s endeavour to find what he wanted at the right moment, became more and more futile, as his clever opponent made point after point successfully, and finally, having listened to numerous chaffing comments on the chaos which had set in, he literally threw away his case by flinging the whole disarranged contents of the carpet bag on the floor, and walking out of the court-house.

BIRKENHEAD.

1851-5.

IN 1851, having obtained the appointment of Engineer-in-Chief at Birkenhead, Mr. Abernethy removed from Aberdeen to reside at 55, Hamilton Square, which he made his head-quarters for some two years. His appointment was chiefly due to the influence of the late Mr. John Laird, M.P., who afterwards became one of his most intimate friends, and to the late Sir Joseph Bailey, Bart., Chairman of the Dock Company, but both at that time, 1851, knew him only by repute as a hydraulic engineer. For four years he acted as engineer to the Birkenhead Dock Trustees, and during that period designed and constructed an extensive range of Graving Docks and River Wall, near Woodside Ferry, in addition to the well-known shipbuilding yard of Messrs. Laird. In

describing the latter work, the *Liverpool Albion*, of
October 21st, 1857, says—

"While inspecting the ship-building yards and works
of Messrs. Laird, the First Lord of the Admiralty,
Sir Charles Wood, appeared to be much struck with
the completeness of the arrangements in every department and with the great engineering skill which
had brought the Graving Docks and the numerous
appliances to such perfection. In justice to
Mr. Abernethy it should be stated that he is entitled
to the chief credit, his plans in every particular having
been closely and faithfully carried out, and at a
marvellously moderate cost."

In 1855, however, the Liverpool Corporation purchased the Birkenhead Company's property, and
Mr. John B. Hartley was appointed engineer in his
place. Later, in 1858, the property was again transferred to the Liverpool Dock Trustees, under the
newly accorded title of the Mersey Docks and Harbour
Board. Before this purchase of the Birkenhead
Company's property by the Liverpool Corporation,
the Birkenhead Dock Company had requested Mr.
Abernethy to design a Dock on the site of Wallasey
Pool, and a rival scheme having been put forward some
years before by one of the most eminent engineers
of the day, the late Mr. James Rendel, he became
involved as one of the principals in a memorable

BIRKENHEAD—MESSRS. LAIRD'S SHIPBUILDING YARD, 1857.

To face page 82.

conflict of engineering opinion which occupied the attention of Parliamentary Committees for a period of twelve years, and although interest in the prolonged engineering controversy has long since abated much of the evidence given is of permanent value as bearing upon the construction of works in the estuary of such a river as the Mersey.

As far back as 1844 Mr. Rendel had brought forward his design for the construction of a Great Float at Birkenhead, and had stated that the first great object he had in view was to give to the Port of Liverpool a Low Water Basin, into which vessels might run as soon as they came up the river from the bar, previous to docking, so as to take away the necessity for dropping anchor, or beating about in the river, to the inconvenience of and danger to one another. The proposed extended accommodation for the Port of Liverpool on the Birkenhead side, was different from any hitherto afforded, or that could be afforded, on the opposite shore as the sills of all the docks at Liverpool were dry at low water spring tides, and only for about two-and-a-half hours of every tide was there available depth for the admission of vessels drawing 18 feet, while at neaps a vessel drawing 16 feet, could not enter any of the docks even at high water. By the proposed Low Water Basin, at Birkenhead, at low water spring tides, vessels drawing 10 feet and at low water neap tides vessels drawing 18 feet would be able to get into dock, while at high water, at neap tides, vessels drawing 29 feet, and at high water of spring tides, vessels drawing 36 feet, would be able to enter without delay.

By Mr. Rendel's scheme, the inner portion of Wallasey Pool was to be converted into a great reservoir, from which sufficient back water might be obtained by retaining the water at the height of the tide of the day by means of an embankment across the Pool, called the Great Dam, in which were situate the tide gates through which vessels would sail into the Great Float above at high water; the smaller gates being used for filling the Pool as the tide rose.

The Low Water Basin proposed to be constructed at the Mersey end of Wallasey Pool was nothing more or less than a long narrow creek, projecting at right angles from the river Mersey, and surrounded on three sides by strong and lofty walls of masonry. The advantage of this proposed basin was, as already stated, that it could be freely used by steamers at the lowest period of low water, and accordingly a floating landing stage was recessed along its southern wall. But the difficulty which militated against the theory was that the silt with which the water of the Mersey is so largely charged would begin to deposit itself when within the still water enclosure, as it had done in the basins on the Liverpool shore, and ultimately render the basin useless by filling up that which had been excavated at so large a cost. To obviate this a system of gigantic sluices were suggested, which by communicating with the Great Float drew off thence sufficient of the superfluous water to scour the basin, and all other works were made subservient to this object.

Such was the scheme put forward in favour of treating Wallasey Pool as a Great Float and Low Water Basin.

In November, 1850, however, a scheme which found favour with some of the Trustees of the Birkenhead Docks was brought forward by Mr. Abernethy, who had on three distinct occasions, dating from 1847, as the Surveying Officer of the Admiralty under the Preliminary Inquiries Act, inspected and reported upon the advisability of providing dock works at Wallasey Pool. In December of that year he produced a plan which was the forerunner of various others projected and recommended in reports, but abandoned almost as scon as ushered into existence.

At length, in April, 1851, he furnished a design which the Trustees thought fit to propose to the Authorities for their sanction, and a letter dated the 26th of April, from the Secretary of the Trustees, accompanied with plans and reports of Messrs. G. Rennie, Captain Maughan, Dock Master of the London Docks, and Captain Andrews, Harbour Master at Lowestoft, was forwarded to the Commissioners for the Conservancy of the Mersey, namely, the First Lord of the Admiralty (Sir F. Baring), the Chancellor of the Duchy of Lancaster, and the Chief Commissioner of Woods. Their lordships took the subject into consideration on the 3rd, 7th, 10th, 14th and 16th of May, and after hearing the explanations of the authors of the two rival schemes, ordered the whole case to be referred to Admiral Sir F. Beaufort and Robert Stephenson, Esq., M.P., if they would undertake the reference.

These gentlemen held a long enquiry, and reported on October 17th, 1851, in favour of Mr. Rendel's scheme, which after further Parliamentary fights in 1852 and 1855 was sanctioned in 1856, and the works of the Great Float were shortly afterwards commenced and finished in 1864.

Passing over the years during which the work was in progress, the *Liverpool Daily Post* of January 21st, 1864, contained the following paragraph :—" Yesterday was a day that will have for the scientific world a peculiar interest. The great sluicing operations at the Birkenhead Low Water Basin, in connection with the Cheshire estate of the Mersey Docks and Harbour Board were commenced. The reputation of a great man, now deceased, was at stake : and the question as to whether Parliament had compelled the Dock Board to expend

£150,000 on a worthless scheme was involved." Some
of the sluices were worked that day without mishap,
but the same paper in its issue of the 26th, had to convey the following tale of disaster.—" The experiments
in connection with the sluicing operations at the Great
Low Water Basin at Birkenhead were resumed
yesterday evening, and we regret to say that a very
serious accident occurred. The works were very much
damaged. . . . At twenty minutes to five the two sluices
at the river end of the 240 feet lock were opened, and
soon gave evidence from the muddy state of the water
that they were doing their work effectually, viz : clear-
ing away the accumulation of silt at the lock entrance.
A few minutes later Mr. Lyster, the dock engineer,
ordered two or three of the cloughs at the head of
the basin to be partially opened, and it having been
ascertained that all was in good order, and the
machinery under perfect control, the whole of the
cloughs were raised and a fierce tide swept along the
basin at the rate of about three miles an hour, carrying
with it a dense body of silt, if one might form a judgment on the subject, from the colour of the water
in the creek. Whilst this operation was proceeding,
it was announced that the two grandest sights in
connection with the experiments were the indraught
of water through the flood gates in the Great Float
into the subterranean chambers below where the spec-

tators were standing, and the regurgitation of the water, caused by its sudden stoppage at the outfall of the sluices by the cloughs or paddles being suddenly closed. . . . These gates are opened and closed by hand power, and when opened are recessed in the walls. It was never intended that they should be secured by anything else than the strong chains by which they are opened and closed, because it was anticipated that the entrances to the floodgate locks being bell-shaped would so direct the water that there would be little, if any, pressure upon the gates. From the commencement of these experiments, however, Mr. Lyster, the dock engineer, somewhat doubting the efficacy of the theory of the engineers who had devised the plans for this portion of the dock works, caused powerful tackle to be placed around the outer head of each gate, so that when opened each pair should be firmly held back in its place. Mr. Lyster was at the southern flood-gate lock explaining to Alderman Woodruff and other gentlemen the reason for adopting this precaution, when a loud grinding noise was heard, followed by a heavy crash. The southern gate of the north flood-gate lock was seen sliding off the coping of the lockpit, and a fearful upheaval of water followed. About 100 ladies and gentlemen ran for their lives, and the greatest consternation was caused by the event. In a few seconds the other gate was lifted slowly for-

ward, the first part to yield apparently being the heel at
the bottom of the gate, then the gate was wrenched off
the massive upper pivot on which it swung, rose about
six feet above the coping, and with a fearful crash fell
into the lock. Both gates were for a second or two
tossed about, and then borne away out of sight by the
swift current—which we likened on Thursday last to a
miniature Niagara above the Falls—into the vast subterranean chambers beneath. . . ."

"On the 23rd of November the water was pumped out
of the north chamber, and an examination showed that
the masonry therein had sustained considerable damage.
The side walls and upper portions of the interior were
uninjured, but a large quantity of the floor at the back
of the sluices had been torn up, and the concrete and
piles laid bare in several places. No remains of the
broken up masonry were found in the chamber; all
had been carried out into the basin except one sandstone ashlar block, which being too large for the opening, had become jammed in one of the central sluices."
These test operations clearly proved that the sluicing
was attended by a considerable amount of danger. It
threatened to destroy the foundations, and by forming
a sub-communication between the Great Float and
the Low Water Basin, to point to the ultimate
destruction of the works. The rapid lowering of the
water, too, in the Great Float was highly objectionable,

for the Low Water Basin had to be cleared of vessels
when the sluices were to be run, and delay arose on
this account. Upon the failure of these great works,
which had occupied the attention of Parliament for
many sessions, a new era opened for Birkenhead, and
in 1866 Mr. Hartley applied to Parliament for powers
to abandon the works, though it was not till after long
negotiations with railway companies and other public
bodies that the authority of Parliament for the abandonment of the great work was obtained.

The preamble of the Act of 1866, after reciting the
section of the Act of 1858, authorizing the construction
of the Low Water Basin, proceeds :—

" And whereas the said works have been completed
and opened for public use, but the operation of the
sluices constructed in accordance with the provisions
of the said Act has been found to be dangerous to the
stability of the works, and practically unsuited to the
proper and efficient working of the Great Float and
Low Water Basin for dock purposes, and it is
therefore necessary that the use of such basin for
the purposes intended by the said Act should be
abandoned, and it is expedient in order to utilize as
far as possible the large amount of money expended
upon the works, that the said Low Water Basin
should be converted into a Wet Dock, so as to be
used in connection with the Great Float, by the

construction of a sea wall at the eastern end of such basin."

Mr. Abernethy's plan as to the best method of utilising Wallesey Pool was with slight alterations adopted. Instead of the water being reduced to and retained at as low a level as possible, as had been planned by Mr. Rendel, it was henceforth to be reduced as little and retained at as high a level as possible. The Great Float was to be a dock, not a reservoir. Mr. Rendel, it is true, had after 1848 regarded the Great Float as a dock, but had designed the latter for maintaining the Great Low Water Basin. "The difference between one plan and the other simply amounted to this: whether the dock is to be designed for maintaining the Great Low Water Basin or creek of the Mersey, or whether the creek of the River Mersey is to be curtailed in its proportions and the dock maintained." * Sluicing was, in the event of silting taking place, to be superseded by a system of dredging, while as substitutes for the tide gates as entrances to the Great Float there was to be a system of entrances by which vessels could be locked up at all times into the Float.

Thus the Low Water Basin, insisted on by Parliament, was still a prominent feature in the scheme, although altered in form and considerably reduced in

* Mr. Abernethy's evidence before the Committee of the House of Commons, May 14th, 1852.

size. Its position on the foreshore remained nearly the same as at first, and it still lay at right angles to the river, but the southern fork was lopped off, and it now took the form of a single channel 1700 feet in length, 400 feet wide at the western end, and 300 feet in width at the mouth. Its primary object, too, was maintained : viz., to serve as an open deep water harbour into which vessels might run and remain, or be "locked" at once into the Float. With the completion of these works, the concluding advice of Mr. Abernethy in his report to the Birkenhead Dock Trustees of May 19th, 1851, in criticism of the Great Low Water Basin scheme was in effect carried out. "The simple and rational course," said he, " to be pursued under existing circumstances appears to me to be to regard the dock as being what it really is—a dock, and to provide a suitable entrance or entrances into it as early as possible, and at the smallest possible cost, in order to develop the germ of traffic already established there at the earliest possible period."

Among the eminent engineers who appeared as witnesses before the Parliamentary Committee for the Bill of 1856 were the late Mr. George Rennie, Sir John Macneill, and Mr. Thomas Hawkesley, in support of the scheme brought forward by Mr. Hartley, and which was in its main features the same as that recommended in 1850 and 1851. In opposition Mr. Rendel very

ably tendered the engineering evidence as he had
done in furtherance of his own scheme in previous
years, while in the list of the leading Counsel engaged
appear the names of Serjeants Bellasis, Wrangham
and Merewether, and Messrs. Hope Scott, Talbot
and T. Webster, father of Sir R. E. Webster, Q.C.,
the present Attorney-General.

BLYTH.

1855-61.

THE Port of Blyth is situated on the coast of Northumberland, about ten miles north of the River Tyne. The surrounding district is rich in coal, but until 1861 only a small class of vessels could trade to the port, and consequently a great part of the coal raised in the neighbourhood was transmitted by rail to the Tyne for shipment. In 1853, however, a Company, of which the Lord of the Manor, Sir M. W. Ridley, father of the present Baronet, Sir M. W. Ridley, Secretary of State for the Home Department, was Chairman, was formed, and powers obtained for improving the harbour, and Mr. Abernethy was appointed Engineer for the works. For a length of a mile the River Blyth was exposed to the action of the sea—a very heavy sea at times—and no vessel could then lie in this portion of what is now the harbour.

Along the seaward side of the river there is a rocky reef called the Coble Hole Rocks, and upon the base thus provided by nature the breakwater was erected. The channel was extremely tortuous, and in many places dry at spring tides. Generally there was not more than a foot of water within it, and a spit of sand extended from the southern side nearly across the entrance, which presented a dangerous obstruction to shipping during rough weather. The channel for its entire length of 4500 feet ran parallel with a lee shore, exposed to the direct action of the north-easterly seas, and consequently scarcely a winter passed without vessels being stranded and wrecked on the beach on the southern side, while the estuary within the river mouth, forming the harbour, was exposed to the sea during on-shore winds.

Guided largely by experience acquired at Aberdeen, which is very similarly situated, he designed works calculated to effect the following objects:—Firstly, to afford protection to vessels entering and leaving from the action of the sea during north-easterly winds; Secondly, to confine and direct the outgoing current, so as to produce sufficient scouring power to maintain the increased depth by dredging; Thirdly, to prolong the outgoing current seaward, so as to bring the detritus carried by it within the influence of the tidal current along the coast.

The works were commenced in 1855 and were completed during 1861, at a total cost of £67,320. They comprised an eastern breakwater 4500 feet in length, a western half-tide training wall 4000 feet in length, and the straightening and deepening of the channel by dredging. Their efficiency soon became apparent after completion. The outgoing current was increased to a velocity of five knots per hour at its greatest strength, whereas, formerly, it was lost immediately on passing the line of the foreshore.

The bar, too, or spit of sand across the entrance entirely disappeared, and a depth of eight or nine feet at low water opposite the breakwater was provided. The channel was further deepened to the extent of four feet, and vessels, after passing within the breakwater, were effectually protected from north-easterly winds.

That the works were considered wholly satisfactory when completed the subjoined letter perhaps affords the best evidence :—

"BLYTH,

"*May* 13*th*, 1862.

"BLYTH HARBOUR.

"DEAR SIR,

"At a Meeting of the Directors of the Blyth Harbour and Dock Company held here to-day, the following Resolution was passed :—

"'A Letter from Mr. Abernethy to Sir M. W. Ridley having

been laid before the Board, in which he intimated that all the works which require his superintendence as at present contemplated by the Company will be completed in the course of a month, it was resolved that this Board beg to record their sense of the zeal and ability with which he has designed and carried out the works, and to request that after the expiration of the present half-year he will consent to act as Consulting Engineer of the Company.'

" I am, Dear Sir,
" Yours very truly,
" JOHN LAWS,
" Secretary.

" James Abernethy, Esq., C.E."

SILLOTH.
1856-9.

The Port of Silloth, in Cumberland, lies on the margin of a small bay on the Southern side of the Solway Frith, twelve miles from Port Carlisle, and thirty miles from the mouth of the estuary. For centuries Silloth Bay has been known as a place of anchorage, and haven of safety for an extensive range of coast. Situated below all the difficult and intricate portion of the navigation of the Solway Firth, with deep water close in shore (an advantage possessed by no other harbour on the Cumberland coast), it was obviously a most desirable site for the construction of a commercial harbour, and had been for a long period considered as such when, in 1854, a company was formed with Mr. William Marshall, M.P., as its Chairman, and an Act obtained for the construction of floating docks, a pier, and other works, in connection with a line of railway, to form a junction with the then existing Port Carlisle Line, which would bring Silloth within twenty-one miles of the City of Carlisle. In the previous Session the Bill had been rejected, owing principally to the strong engineering and nautical evidence tendered in opposition. But the temporary reverse experienced by the promoters was upon the whole beneficial, as it caused them to carefully reconsider their scheme, and in the Bill of the following year a better site was selected. The general design for the works was prepared by the late Mr. John Hartley, whose other duties at Birkenhead necessitated his resignation as engineer after the passing of the Act, and his successor was Mr. Abernethy. The works were carried out in accordance with the general arrangement of the original design. This consisted of a pier or jetty 1,000 feet in length on the seaward side of the dock entrance: an entrance channel parallel with the jetty, forming a slight angle with the foreshore, 100 feet in width at the bottom, with slopes of six to one, having a fall of two feet six inches in its entire length, the bottom of the channel being generally sixteen feet below the level of the adjoining beach : thirdly, an enbankment on the foreshore, projecting 400 feet beyond high water mark, and enclosing the entrance to the dock, sixty feet in width, and securing a depth of twenty-four feet of water over the sill at high water ordinary spring tides. Reverse, or sea-gates also were erected for protection during gales : and lastly, a dock of four acres with a depth of water of twenty-five feet six inches at the general level.

Operations were commenced in 1856, and completed in 1859 at a total cost of £122,000, and were opened in August, 1859, by the then First Lord of the Admiralty, Sir James Graham.

The construction of the dock was a work of considerable difficulty, inasmuch as a strong artificial foundation had to be made in sand of great depth and of a light quality in order to support the masonry.

PORTPATRICK.

1858-64.

DURING the same period—1855-61—he was also engaged in improving the harbours of Watchett in Somersetshire, Lossiemouth in Elgin, and Stranraer and Portpatrick in the Rhinns of Galloway on the south west corner of Scotland. At Stranraer he made the acquaintance of Sir John Ross, the celebrated Arctic navigator, and used to visit him at his house called "North-West Castle," where he had a dining room fitted to represent the interior of a ship's cabin. His friendship with Sir James and his brother Alexander Caird also began while these last-named works were in progress.

The improvements at Portpatrick were undertaken in the month of July, 1858, on appointment by the Lords Commissioners of the Admiralty, with the view of establishing a short sea passage between Scotland and Ireland, in connection with the railways at that time in course of construction towards that port. The

works proposed, which were sufficient to meet the
requirements of the contemplated service to Donag-
hadee in Ireland, comprised the formation of a channel
120 feet in width, with a depth of 10 feet at low water,
spring tides, requiring 9,789 cubic yards of excavation,
and a tidal basin of one and one eighth of an acre,
including the excavation of 65,000 cubic yards, with
an entrance 75 feet in width, and of a corresponding
depth to the entrance channel, at a cost of £19,490,
and a pier extension formed of large blocks of masonry
at a further sum of £16,943. The undertaking was
successfully completed at the end of 1864, and although,
as will be gathered from the dimensions given, it
was comparatively small : it was, nevertheless, one
of considerable difficulty in execution in consequence
of the very exposed situation of the port, and the
heavy seas to which the works were constantly subjected while in course of progression, while much of
the deepening had to be effected through hard rock.

SWANSEA.

1849-93.

T HE natural advantages of the Port of Swansea, from its position at the entrance of the Bristol Channel, with an excellent roadstead at the Mumbles, and in close contiguity to the great coal fields of South Wales, could not fail to recommend it as a port capable of very extensive development as soon as the exigencies of trade might demand it, and the Harbour Trustees in the year 1849, of whom Mr. Pascoe St. Leger Grenfell was chairman, realized the necessity for providing further and better accommodation for the steadily increasing trade of the Port, and applied to Mr. Abernethy, whom they had consulted two years before with respect to prospective improvements, to make a report and to prepare a design, and appointed him their Engineer-in-Chief for the contemplated works

in May of that year. Being at the time resident in
Aberdeen, the additional appointment at Swansea necessitated frequent long journeys by coach viâ Edinburgh,
Newcastle, Birmingham, and Gloucester, a distance of
over five hundred miles. Swansea at that date—1849
—contained but thirty thousand inhabitants, and the
only harbour works in existence were a few quays built
along the banks of the River Tawe, alongside of which
vessels floated or lay dry, as the tide flowed or ebbed,
but the bed of the river was very uneven, and vessels
as they grounded were liable to be strained. Finding
such to be the condition of the harbour in 1849, the
Engineer recommended the Harbour Trustees to construct a floating basin in the bed of the River Tawe on
a plan similar to that previously adopted at Bristol and
" The Pent," at Dover, a somewhat favourite scheme
during the first half of the present century. A bend
of the Tawe was cut off and converted into the North
Dock, or Town Float, this being really a portion of
the old river bed locked and floated, the fresh water
from the interior being carried to the sea by a side
cut. This North Dock, which the accompanying illustration shows to be situated on the left or western side
of the River, and the furthest dock from the River
mouth, has an area of ten and a quarter acres, and
a half-tide basin of two and a half acres. It was completed in 1852, and its beneficial effect, jointly with the

extension of the railway to the docks in 1853 was mani
fested by the rise of the tonnage entering the port from
270,000 tons in 1851 to 332,000 tons in 1853.   It
was during the construction of the lock at the entrance
of this North Dock that Mr. Abernethy first suggested
to the Harbour Trustees the desirability of working
the gates by hydraulic power instead of by the usual
hand gear.   Sir William Armstrong was applied to,
and, as the result of an interview with the Trustees,
designed the machinery.   The increase of trade continued steady and rapid, and in 1858 amounted in
round numbers to 500,000 tons.   Of this, the increase
in the foreign trade alone was from 60,000 tons to
262,000 tons.

The chief export trade from Swansea is, of course,
coal, of which 267,430 tons were shipped in 1858, and
an additional quantity coastways of 185,712 tons.
There was also at that date a large export of patent
fuel—a manufacture for many years peculiar to Swansea
—to all quarters of the world, and a large importation
of copper ore from Cornwall, South America, Cuba,
and Australia, the copper smelting business carried on
then representing nearly nine-tenths of the copper
smelting business of the world.

Such a thriving trade as this promised speedily to
outgrow the accommodation provided in 1852, and it
became necessary to look for some means of extending

the harbour. Before the formation of the River Float
in 1852, a project had been started for building new
docks on the west side of the river near its entrance,
and nearly at right angles to the North Dock, and a
Company was formed for that purpose. An Act also was
obtained for its construction, and operations were commenced, but for some reason or other the Harbour
Trustees did not associate themselves with the scheme,
but preferred to persevere with the Floating Basin,
which they finished with their own funds. If their
refusal was grounded on a suspicion that the Company
would not be able to perform their programme, they
were justified by the event, for after a few years funds
became scarce, the works languished, and at last after
an expenditure of £100,000 came to a standstill. In
this condition they remained for three years, until the
Trustees came to terms with the insolvent Company,
and took the unfinished works off their hands, again
deputing Mr. Abernethy to act as their engineer, who
placed Mr. William Neill there as Resident Engineer,
the Contractor being Mr. William Tredwell.

In making this dock, one of the first operations
was the formation of an embankment for the purpose
of excluding the sea ; timber groynes were constructed
at intervals of 1500 feet to the full extent of the proposed embankment. The rough boulder gravel found
immediately under the sand and the made ground was

then tipped between the groynes at the seaward end,
the lighter material being deposited within and towards
the landward end.   The action of the sea and the tide
removed the lighter portion of the gravel, and carried
it to the westward, leaving the heavier portion and the
boulder stones to gradually form a beach and serve as
a facework to the embankment, and this proved an
effective barrier to the encroachment of the sea.

The successful application of hydraulic machinery
for working the lock of the North Dock and Newport
Dock (page 166), where the gates were much heavier,
induced the engineer to adopt a similar system for
the entrance to this new dock, and Sir William Armstrong & Co. again supplied all the requisite machinery for opening and shutting the gates, bridges, and
sluices, as well as for turning the capstans.   Hydraulic
coal hoists which had shortly before proved a great
success at Newport were also supplied by the same
firm of mechanical engineers and erected upon the
quay.

The new dock taken in hand on the west side of the
entrance of the river was called the South Dock, consisting of an outer basin of thirteen acres, with 4,800 feet
of quay wall, and an inner basin of four acres with a
quay wall of 1,600 feet, these two basins communicating
with each other by means of a lock 300 feet by 60 feet.

The old high water mark ran through the centre of

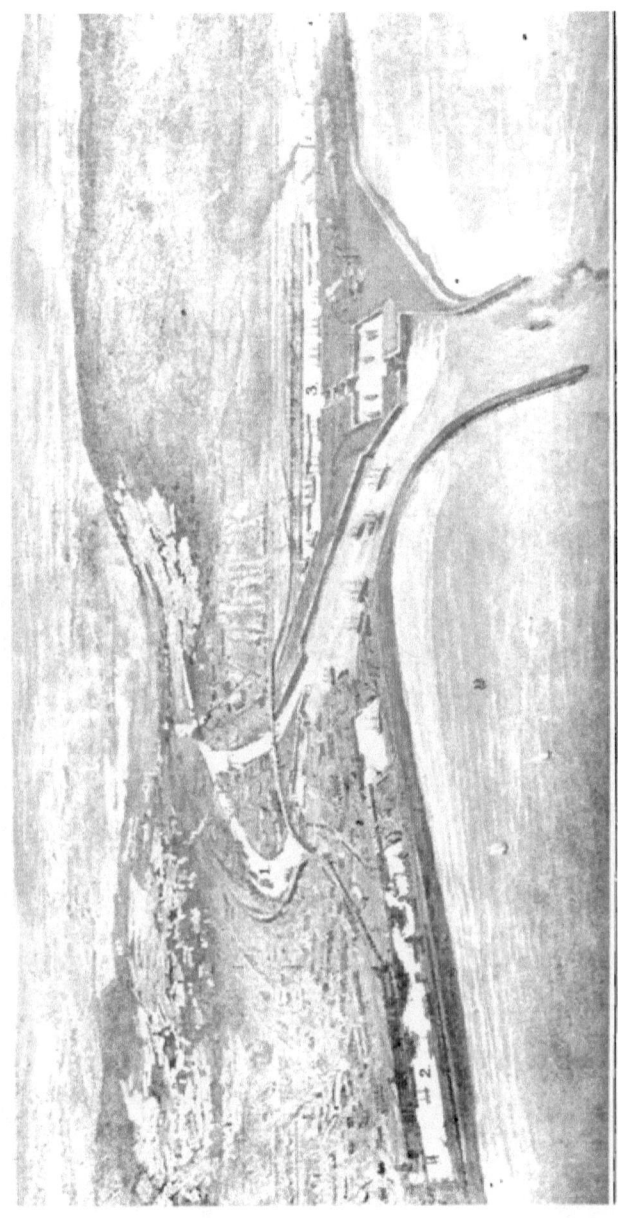

SWANSEA DOCKS.

1. North Dock, 1852   2. South Dock, 1858.   3. Prince of Wales' Dock, 1881.

the dock and lock, so that one half of the area enclosed was reclaimed from the sea, and by this reclamation the once fashionable Swansea Sands disappeared, but Mr. Clark Russell has well expressed the view entertained by the inhabitants with regard to such a change when he wrote of Swansea in 1882 :—" One must not think of the beautiful, but of the useful, with a capital U. Nobody talks of sea views or mountains here, but of how many ships were cleared last week, and what the export and import returns were and the like."

After the completion of the South Dock, which was opened by Miss Talbot, daughter of the Lord Lieutenant of the County of Glamorgan, in 1858, at a cost of £169,073, the export and import trades continued to grow apace, and in 1872 the then Mayor, Mr. James Livingstone, advocated the construction of a third dock on the east side of the river Tawe. The Act for this large addition to the Port was obtained in 1874, and in March, 1880, Sir H. Vivian, afterwards Lord Swansea, laid the central stone of the lock amid demonstrations of great enthusiasm. The work involved the removal of 2,000,000 cubic yards of earth and the building of 80,000 cubic feet of masonry, at a cost of half a million sterling. The dock area is twenty-three acres, the depth on the outer sill of the lock being thirty-two feet at ordinary tides, and that over the inner sill twenty-seven feet, while the Tidal Basin by which it is approached has an area of four and a half acres.

It will be remembered that in the account of the life and work at Aberdeen at page 70, mention was made of Mr. Abernethy having been deputed to superintend the arrangements for the disembarkation of Her Majesty the Queen on the occasion of her first visit to Scotland in September, 1848, and it is a coincidence worthy of mention that on the occasion of the first visit of T.R.H. the Prince and Princess of Wales to South Wales thirty-three years afterwards to open the Prince of Wales' Dock he was again appointed to receive and conduct the Royal Party to inspect the gates and masonry of the lock, prior to requesting the Prince to touch the lever which was to open the gates, and the Princess to sever the white ribbon by which act the suspended bottle of champagne fell and christened the dock The Prince of Wales' Dock. The *Daily News* of October 19th, 1881, gives His Royal Highness's speech at the banquet, part of which runs thus :—" It has long been the wish of the Princess and myself to have some public occasion of visiting the Principality, from which we are proud to derive our title, and we are particularly glad that *our first visit to South Wales* should be connected with the opening of these docks at Swansea."

In concluding his speech, His Royal Highness com-

plimented Mr. Abernethy, President of the Institution
of Civil Engineers, upon the successful termination of
his professional labours as the engineer.

The late Mr. T. A. Walker, who afterwards made
the Severn Tunnel, acted as contractor and completed
the work in the remarkably short space of two-and-
a-half years.

The population of Swansea had increased in 1881
from 10,000 in 1852 to 100,000, and the town become
the metallurgical centre of the world, the district
abounding in large and busy works, at which some
20,000 hands were employed in the production in
marketable form of iron, patent fuel, copper, tin
plates, steel spelter, silver, lead, zinc, nickel, sulphate
of ammonia, oxalic acid, cobalt, ultramarine, &c., and
the gross income from imports had reached 67 per cent.,
and from exports 64 per cent.

In the year 1885 the tonnage in the Prince of Wales'
Dock amounted to 623,280 tons, and the revenue from
it till June of that year £39,227, while the working ex-
penses and maintenance amounted to but 37 per cent.,
while the gross income of the Harbour Trustees had
risen from £5,000 in 1851 to £100,000 in 1886. It is a circumstance worth noticing that no grant of public money
has ever been made in respect of improving the Port of
Swansea. In addition to the construction of the
Prince of Wales' Dock, the West Pier was lengthened

from 600 feet to 1,000 feet, an East Pier built. and the
approach channel deepened to 28 feet at high water
ordinary tides.

In 1893 he again prepared plans for a new dock at
Swansea, completing thereby a professional association
with the port of forty-six years duration.

FALMOUTH.

1860-3.

FOR a period of 180 years, from 1688 to 1850, with the exception of an interval of a few months, Falmouth was the Mail Packet Station of the Kingdom, and thence mails were despatched periodically to Lisbon, Cadiz, Oporto, Gibraltar, and the Mediterranean, Halifax, New York, Bermuda, Barbadoes, Jamaica, and the other West Indian Islands, Mexico and the Havannah, Brazil and Buenos Ayres. In this service some thirty-nine sailing packets were employed, and for some years after the majority of them had been superseded by steamers, Falmouth continued to be the Mail Packet Station of the Post Office for the despatch of mails to America and the West Indies.

As far back as the year 1838, the Government had

contracted with a Company, of which Mr. Cunard was
Chairman, for the conveyance of the North American
Mails from Liverpool, and a further contract was made
in 1842 with the Peninsula and West India Companies
for the transport of the West Indian and Mexican
Mails from Southampton, but these mails were still, by
the terms of the contract, embarked and landed at
Falmouth. It was alleged, however, that Falmouth
did not possess railway communication, and that the
great increase of commerce rendered it necessary that
the Mail Packet Station should be at some port
possessing that advantage.

The Peninsula and West India Companies also
exhibited a strong desire to be absolved from the
arrangement which compelled them to call at Falmouth, instead of steaming direct to the more eastern
port of Southampton, and endeavoured to influence the
Government to concede that point in their favour. In
the year 1840 a Commission was appointed by the
Admiralty to examine the ports of the English Channel,
and to recommend the one in their judgment the
most suitable for a Packet Station. Dartmouth was
the port selected, but the House of Commons refused to accept the choice, and appointed a Committee to undertake the duty afresh. This Committee,
after a long enquiry, reported, " That having
proceeded with the utmost diligence in the examination

of witnesses to establish the capabilities and relative merits of different ports for the service embraced by the order of the House, and the subject of the contract before mentioned, they present the following resolutions as their opinion upon the evidence :—

"Resolved : That, notwithstanding the port of Dartmouth has been recommended by the Committee, appointed by the Admiralty, as the port of departure and arrival of the West India mail packet, this Committee are not prepared to recommend that Dartmouth should be selected for that service.

"That they consider a western port most desirable for landing and embarking the mails to and from the West Indies, and that provided a railway existed to the southwest of Land's End, and a harbour was constructed in that neighbourhood where the mails might with facility be put on board and landed, they would unhesitatingly recommend that harbour to their lordship's adoption."

They thought it "proper to premise, that in a selection of a western port for a station for the delivery and reception of the West Indian mails, in preference to one situated more to the eastward, they took into account the greater degree of uncertainty which is attached to the transport of mails by steam vessels compared with that in which a coach or railroad becomes the medium of conveyance; and as it respects

I

the eastern port, it should be borne in mind that the correspondence to and from the western part of our shores would be subject to a carriage in both cases, by sea and land, very wide of their destination."

The witnesses examined, and upon whose evidence the report of the Committee was largely based, were officers of high standing in Her Majesty's Navy and representatives of the Post Office, and both the Admiralty and the Post Office were in favour of retaining Falmouth as the Packet Station for the West India Mail Service. The Treasury, however, eventually yielded to the influence brought to bear upon it in favour of Southampton, and in September, 1843, the carrying Companies were permitted to embark and land mails at the latter port. In 1850 the mail service to Madeira and Brazil was also withdrawn, and Falmouth ceased altogether to be a Packet Station, and so lost a branch of Government patronage which it had enjoyed for nearly two centuries. The mails were transferred to Southampton and Liverpool, from which two ports they continue to be sent.

It was not, however, it will be observed, until great pressure had been brought to bear on the Government of the day that the transference was accomplished. It was admitted that as regards geographical position and the extent and excellence of her harbour, Falmouth stood unrivalled as a mail station. It could be entered at all states of the tide by the largest vessels in almost any wind, and when once they got inside they were as safe as in a dock. In addition to this, vessels stopping there would avoid the delay and dangers of the further channel navigation to the Solent of some 200 miles, and thence up the narrow and crowded Southampton Water for a distance of another ten miles, before the Port of Southampton is reached. In point of time, some ten hours, at least, would, it was maintained be easily saved in the delivery and transmission of mails to London, if a direct railway communication extended to Falmouth, and it was further thought that the majority of passengers arriving from abroad would gladly avail themselves of the earliest opportunity of terminating their voyage.

There was good reason to expect, therefore, that with improved harbour accommodation and a through line of railway to London, the absence of which had been the only real disadvantage urged against the port by the Peninsula and West India Companies, and the importance of constructing which had been recognised by the Committee of the House of Commons, a portion, at any rate, of the lost patronage would return; and upon the many grounds of its large area and safety as a harbour, increased expedition, public convenience, and facility of communication by the extension of the Cornwall Railway from Truro to Falmouth, which

I 2

was duly opened on August 22nd, 1863, the Directors of the Falmouth Docks, of whom Mr. Baring, M.P. for Falmouth and Penryn, (Lord Northbrook) was Chairman, confidently anticipated that Falmouth would again one day become what her position and great natural capabilities pre-eminently qualified her to be, the great mail packet station, or perhaps even as Earl St. Vincent, when First Lord of the Admiralty at the beginning of the century, predicted, "the general, free and warehousing port of all England," and obtained the sanction of Parliament to construct there large and efficient docks.

The surface area of Falmouth harbour is upwards of nine square miles. Of this the principal part is the great anchorage of Carrick Road, four nautical miles in length, and, on an average, one in breadth. On the western side and just within the entrance, which is a mile in width, is the inner harbour, an oval land-locked basin, formerly the anchorage of the packets, with the town of Falmouth on the southern shore, and Flushing opposite. A creek extends from the upper part for about a mile-and-a-half beyond these towns, at the head of which is the ancient borough of Penryn, noted for its large granite works. Various other creeks run inland from the harbour making up a total shore mileage of some seventy miles.

The inner harbour is a nearly land-locked basin to

FALMOUTH HARBOUR AND GRAVING DOCKS, 1863.

To face page 117.

the west of Carrick Road, and immediately at the back
of Pendennis Hill. It opens from Carrick Road with
a breadth of 1,000 yards measured from Bar Point,
the northern extremity of Pendennis to Trefusis Point
opposite. Its greatest breadth from a deep bight
inside the Bar Point to Kiln Quay, Trefusis, is three-
quarters of a mile, and from this it gradually narrows
to about 1,000 yards at the Ferry between Falmouth
and Flushing, where it becomes Penryn River.

It was in connection with this inner harbour that
the Falmouth Docks Company, in 1860, invited
Mr. Abernethy to design and execute dock works by
which its natural advantages were further improved,
and rendered in every way available for the requirements of commerce and shipping. Graving docks
were built where large sailing vessels and steamers
might be docked and repaired; and provision made
for landing passengers at the railway terminus, where
the depth of water was such that the largest class of
steamers in those days might lie alongside and cargoes
be shipped, discharged, or warehoused, with the greatest
facility.

These works are situated on the southern side immediately under Pendennis Castle, and within five minutes
steaming of the open sea. A site more admirably
adapted both by reason of its well sheltered position
and its easy access at all times and states of tide

and weather, could scarcely be conceived. The area embraced by the works is about 120 acres, comprising a tidal harbour, floating dock, graving docks, warehouses, etc., and the entrance channel to them is 600 feet in width, with a depth of 18 to 20 feet of water at low water spring tides.

The tidal harbour area exceeds 42 acres, and its depth varies from 23 to 18 feet. It is enclosed on the east side by the Prince of Wales' Breakwater, 1,400 feet in length; on the west, by wharves of about 1,200 feet in length, in the centre of which is the opening to the floating dock; and on the north by a breakwater and wharf 1,500 feet in length, which completes the enclosure with the exception of a space of 450 feet between it and the head of the Prince of Wales' Breakwater. The floating dock is 14 acres in extent, and there are two graving docks, one 400 feet by 35 feet, and the other 350 feet by 50 feet. All these works were executed at a cost of £120,000 within the short space of two years, a result largely due to the supervision of the resident engineer, Mr. J. R. Kellock, and the constant attention and energy which the Chairman, the Directors, and the late Mr. T. H. Tilly, solicitor, displayed from the commencement of operations.

His Royal Highness the late Prince Consort took considerable interest in the Falmouth Dock Bill of

1860, and by special request Mr. Abernethy attended at Buckingham Palace on Sunday, March 4th, 1860, and had the honour of explaining the plans to him. H.R.H. the Prince of Wales was also present at the interview.

ITALY.

TURIN AND SAVONA RAILWAY.

1862-66.

IT was not until the year 1862 that he was called upon to execute any engineering scheme of importance in foreign countries, but during the next four years the scene of his principal work shifted to Italy, Austria, Hungary, and Egypt. The project of the Turin and Savona Railway originated in Italy, and the route had already been carefully selected and surveyed by M. Peyron, and an influential Italian Council of Administration formed, with Signor Rarratri, a Member of the Chamber of Deputies, as Chairman. It was to England, however, that the promoters looked for the raising of the requisite capital, and with the many distinguished names which appeared on the Italian Council, their expectations were in a short time realized and operations commenced. Raising the capital in England naturally involved the formation of an English Committee of Shareholders, and several gen-

tlemen of good position were selected.   Previous
to the formation of the English Committee, however,
the Italian Council had entered into a contract with
certain Italian bankers, Messrs. Guastalla, to construct
the line for the sum of £2,408,000, a premature
arrangement which led to great pecuniary difficulties
before the railway had been completed.

The length of the proposed line, the construction
of which was entrusted to Mr. Abernethy as Engineer-
in-Chief in September, 1862, was 120 miles, traversing
some of the most fertile districts in Piedmont.   Commencing by a junction with the line from Turin and
Carmagnola, it shortly formed further junction with
the lines leading to Alessandria, Milan, and by a new
proposed branch, to Acqui, in Lombardy.   Proceeding
in a southward direction the new main line passed
near Millesimo, the valley of the Bormida, La Sella,
to the Port of Savona, on the Mediterranean, where
it formed a junction with the littoral line leading to
Genoa and Nice, and which was improved and deepened
with a view to meeting the increase of traffic upon the
completion of the railroad.   There were numerous
"works of art" along the route of the line, comprising
viaducts, some thirty in number, which were built of
wrought iron girders, and nine short tunnels of a
total length of 988 yards, and other works of a like
nature on the branch line from Carcari to Acqui, all

of which, however, admitted of easy construction, and call for no special mention, but the two principal works of art of engineering interest were piercing the two long tunnels, La Sella, 4 miles in length, commencing at a point distant some ten miles from Savona, and the Belbo tunnel, exceeding $2\frac{3}{4}$ miles. That of La Sella in the inner range of the Apennines was driven through blue schist clay and soft rock from ten pits sunk at intervals, under the superintendence of Mr. Cay, C.E., the resident engineer on that section, the headings from each pit being driven right and left.   This tunnel had originally been designed in the form of a double curve by M. Peyron, but at Mr. Abernethy's suggestion the curve was entirely abolished, which shortened the work by some 370 metres and lessened the difficulty of correctly carrying the planimetrical course which would have attended the original design.

The Belbo tunnel was pierced principally through soft sandstone rock, and it was anticipated from the nature of the formation, previously ascertained by borings, that the expense of the greater length of drilling compared with the La Sella tunnel would be largely compensated by the absence of water, which as expected had in the latter work impeded operations to a serious extent.   This sanguine hope, however, proved to have been built up on a false character

frequently given to sandstone, and much difficulty
was experienced and delay and expense involved,
owing to the frequent appearance of water, but the
work was very energetically pushed forward and successfully completed by an old pupil and assistant,
Mr. Samuel Brown, C.E., who afterwards, in 1878,
became the Government engineer in Cyprus, and
thence was appointed by Lord Knutsford Surveyor-
General at Hong Kong in 1889, a post which he held
at the time of his death in 1891.

The journey from London to Turin during the years
1862-66 occupied three days and three nights, the railroad communication being at that time completed as
far only as Culoz in Savoy, and the route from this
point onwards had to be continued by diligence *viâ* Aix-
les-Bains, Chambéry, Modane, and over Mont Cenis, a
distance of about 106 miles. Diaries kept during this
period afford evidence that visits to the scene of work
were frequently paid during the winter months, and
when the road was deeply covered with snow. Entries
of date February 13th and 14th, 1863, record one such
experience, and others of January 18th, 19th and 20th
in the preceding year an even more difficult journey,
when sledges had to be requisitioned in place of the
diligence. These, however, became embedded in a
snow drift near the summit of the pass, and were
extricated after considerable delay only to get into a

worse position near No. 5 Casine on the road to Susa, where shortly afterwards the sledge capsized in a snow-drift, and the travellers were compelled to seek shelter for thirty-six hours in the *Casine,* leaving the vehicle and baggage behind to be speedily buried in the drifting snow. While in shelter in the hut they were joined by other refugees from the storm, making up the number of the inmates to sixteen. The second party included some ladies, who were accommodated for the night in a small room usually occupied by the resident *cantonnier* and his wife, while the other apartment of some fifteen feet square was littered with straw as a makeshift for the gentlemen. With the outer door closed the air inside this limited space soon became insufferable, a condition of things which led to some exciting scenes at the time, and afforded amusement on subsequent reflection. Among the row of uncomfortable sleepers was a Scotchman of the name of Dalry, who during the night strongly advocated a replenishing of the heated air by the colder atmosphere from outside. "Man," he said, addressing his compatriot from Aberdeen, "I canna stand the heat, gae and open the door a wee bittie ; " and the latter being the reclining form nearest to the door, complied with the behest and unfastened the bolt. The door only too readily opened with the pressure of the gale against it, and a shower of snow was forthwith admitted, besprinkling the entire

recumbent company. This was naturally followed by
a general outcry in French and Italian accents, and
the door was again with considerable exertion closed
and bolted, but the effect of the sudden inrush of cold
air into the overheated room was to produce a con-
densation which certainly did not make the apartment
any more comfortable. When all had fully expressed
their disapproval of the ill-considered act, and sleep
again taken possession of their limbs, the Scotchman
quietly arose, and stepping lightly over the prostrate
malcontents, soliloquised as he made his way towards
the bolt, "I'll hae that steeked door open again," which
he did with the same consequences as in the first essay,
but on this occasion the exclamations and gesticula-
tions were redoubled, and he wisely abstained from
risking the consequences of a third attempt to obtain
fresh air, and returned to his allotted space on the floor.

On the morning of January 20th, the storm had to
some extent abated, and a chief *cantonnier* with a gang
of men arrived, and cut a passage through the drift and
the party reached Susa at eight o'clock in the evening.

During several of the many visits to inspect the line
of railway in progress of construction, the diaries also
point to the hospitality of Mons. Fortunatus Prandi, at
whose house he not unfrequently used to stay for one
or two days at a time. This house was situated on
high land among the maritime Alps, and from the

drawing-room windows commanded a glorious view
of the Alpine range, with Monte Viso towering into
the clouds capped with snow. But reaching the drawing-room, although on the first floor only, was by no
means an easy matter, for on each of the three landings
which broke the monotony of the broad wooden stair-
case, a bull-dog was chained as a sentry, with full
command (as each of the animals seemed to be well
aware), of the entire range of floor opposite to his
kennel, and these sentries never failed to challenge
any stranger who attempted to pass by.

Mons. Prandi's career had been somewhat remarkable. At the age of seventeen he entered the army,
but having taken a somewhat prominent part in some
insubordinate conduct displayed by students at his
military college at Alessandria, he made a timely
escape to Savona, and there found shelter on an
English collier, which eventually brought him to London. He continued to reside for some years in
London, earning a livelihood by teaching Italian, and
being a man of good birth and address, succeeded in
making friends with several persons of good social
position, among whom Lord Brougham, treated him
very kindly. In 1860 Mons. Prandi returned to his
home, where he died in 1870, and was buried in the
chapel close by his house, in which his brother officiated
as priest.

THE GRAND CAVOUR CANAL.

1862-7.

SIMULTANEOUSLY with the construction of the
Turin and Savona Railway, a large irrigation
work—the Canal Cavour—was in course of progress
in Italy, called after the celebrated Italian statesman
of that name, and Mr. Abernethy held the position
of consulting or "controlling" engineer to the Italian
Irrigation Canal Company, who were carrying out
the undertaking which had been planned in 1854, by
the eminent Government Engineer, Chevalier Noé, and
submitted to the Government of Italy and approved,
but its execution postponed on account of the un-
settled state of the country. The project consisted
in reducing to one system of management, the existing
Crown canals on the left bank of the Po, between the
rivers Orco and Ticino, and in the construction of a

high level canal from the River Po, crossing the Dora
Baltea and the Sesia, and terminating on the Ticino.
To the above company the government now ceded the
Crown Canals for the sum of £812,000, and on this
sum and on the cost of all works connected with the
canals, as well as on the cost of the Canal Cavour,
guaranteed six per cent. with all surplus revenue, for a
period of fifty years. Although the scheme of the
company was apparently divided into different parts, it
had in reality but one great object—namely, to perfect
and increase the means of irrigation in those districts
east of Turin, which lie in the valleys of the Po and
Ticino rivers, and west of Lombardy. The trunk line
was the Grand Cavour Canal, 54 miles long, carried
across the main drainage of the Alps from Chivasso, a
point upon the river Po ten miles east of Turin, to the
Ticino river beyond Novara. The second branch of
the scheme was the acquisition of the Crown lands in
the Ivrea and Vercellise provinces, for incorporation
with the operations in irrigation of the new canal,
and the third branch, the purchase of such private canals
in the Novara province as might be necessary to give
to the trunk canal command of the whole country,
which lies south of Novara between the Sesia and
Ticino rivers. Power was also taken in the concession
given to extend operations into Upper Lombardy,
where a large dry district of 100,000 acres could

be advantageously watered by the resources of the company. The total area to be irrigated was 300,000 acres, and the foundation stone of the Canal Cavour, which was to effect the major part of this drainage, was laid on June 1st, 1863, by Prince Humbert, to whom, previous to the ceremony, Mr. Abernethy was introduced by Mons. Noé. The science of irrigation, as applied in Italy, India, or Egypt, is perhaps little known in England, where counter efforts are more usually made to drain the water from the land in order to render it capable of improved cultivation. In the former countries, on the other hand, the land requires a supply of water in order to develop and fertilise it, and many of the smaller rivers are dry during the summer.

Taking a glance on the map at the physical nature of the tract of country in north Italy, affected by these irrigation works, one can see a striking similarity in the more important features of the land with northern India. Both are situated at the base of mountains of perpetual snow drained by rivers flowing thence: geologically they belong to the same period, and may be said to be generically the same. There is, however, this point of difference, that whereas, in India, the great drainage river has but one range of mountains, the river Po is affected by two ranges, between which it flows at a greater or less angle with its affluents, and thus occupies the lowest level of the valley which it traverses. On the left bank of the Po irrigation had previously been successfully carried out by canals from the various affluents, the Orco, Dora Baltea, Sesia, Agogna, Terdoppio and Ticino, but the Po itself had never been laid under contribution. Large tracts remained starved between the Sesia and the Ticino, while a portion remained utterly waste, and it was to lay the River Po under contribution to this district, and for the systematising of the other works, already alluded to, that the concession was made and the guarantee granted to the Italian Irrigation Company.

In this undertaking, as in the preceding one, there was a good deal of reckless speculation, and considerable misfortune overtook many of the large shareholders, who were no doubt influenced to some extent in their application for shares by the distinguished names which appeared on the Italian Board of Directors, which contained those of the Marquis Cavour, Count Oldepedi, Senator Farrina, and M. de Vicenzie, Minister of Public Works, among others. The English Board of Directors were also gentlemen of good position, one of whom, Colonel Collyer, R.E., became an intimate and valued friend in subsequent years,

The obligation put upon the " controlling " engineer of the Canal was that he should visit the works while in progress every four months, and inspect and advise

upon them, and the report written to the Italian Irrigation Canal Company upon the occasion of the first
compliance with the obligation imposed, shows plainly
that he was dissatisfied with the method of procedure, for
it concludes as follows :—" I regret to state that I was
very much disappointed at the progress of the works,
and more especially with the very inadequate provision
made for their future progress. There is no well considered organization, nor sufficient implements and
machines to ensure their being executed in a given time
and with due economy, and unless this is speedily
remedied it is utterly impossible to define either the
period for the completion of the Canal, or its ultimate
cost."

A short time after this report had been sent to the
Board a letter was received from the Secretary desiring
a personal attendance at Turin for the purpose of
explaining the reasons for having made such a strong
attack on the method of conducting the works. Only
one member of the English Board, Colonel Collyer,
consented to accompany the engineer, who on June
20th, 1864, before a full meeting of the Italian Board,
explained, through the medium of Dr. Gallen, an
English physician resident in Italy, who acted as
interpreter, the various unsatisfactory arrangements
which in his judgment warranted the wording of the
report. The explanation was apparently followed by

K 2

satisfactory results, for the Marquis Cavour subsequently called and expressed his appreciation of the
reasons given, and the contractor employed M.
Tatti, an engineer of Milan, to supervise the works
in progress, and under the last named gentleman and
the staff of resident engineers, chief among whom was
Mr. More, C.E., now Engineer-in-Chief to the Thames
Conservancy Board, the works were successfully completed. Mr. Abernethy made several visits to Venice
while the Canal Cavour was in progress, and upon one
occasion made a sketch, which is reproduced on the
opposite page.

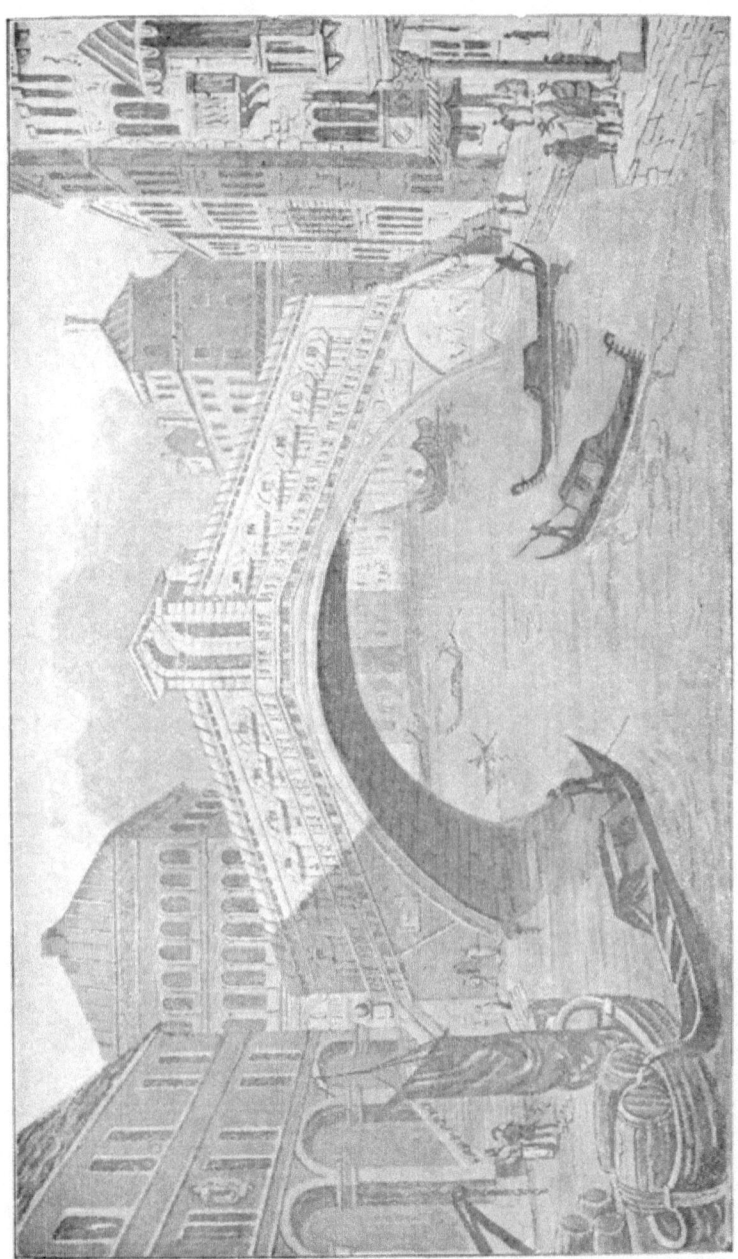

PONTE DI RIALTO, VENICE.

To face page 132.

AUSTRIA.

1866-8.

HAVING completed a periodical inspection of the Canal Cavour, early in January, 1866, he proceeded to Vienna at the request of Count Apponyi, the Austrian Ambassador in London, who had invited him to become a member of the Commission, under the presidency of General Baron Scholl, to be appointed to consider and report upon the regulation of the River Danube at that City, and which, subsequently to his visit, he accepted. The Commission consisted of four expert engineers, in addition to Baron Scholl, viz :— Messrs. James Abernethy, of London, G. Hagen, of Berlin, M. Sexauer, of the Grand Duchy of Baden, and A. Tostain, Director General of the Southern Railway of Vienna. All information referring to the improvement of the Danube was given to the Commissioners by the Minister of the Interior, Count Taaffe, in Vienna, where lengthy discussions took place later in the year at various meetings, but the opinions of the engineers, not being sufficiently harmonious to admit of signing a joint report, it was decided that each, independently, should submit his recommendation as to the best method of effecting the improvement of the Danube. This was accordingly done, the London engineer advising the construction of preliminary works in the form of groynes or jetties at an acute angle with the river bank, so as to direct the main current towards the centre of the channel, and generally to lessen curvature. When the bed of the river had become more regular and deeper, as the effect of having made these groynes, to proceed in the next place, to form fixed or continuous banks. It was further recommended to change the course of the river opposite to the City with a view to facilitating the discharge of flood waters. Extensive embankments were to be raised to protect the city and country in the vicinity from inundation, the material for them being obtained by the excavation from the proposed new channel. Lastly, to construct regulating works at the head of the Donan Canal, so as to supply a fixed and adequate flow at all times without risk of inundation or interference with the navigation between it and the river, a lock for the passage of vessels from the canal into the river, and an additional short canal between the two last mentioned, the estimate for the entire work being given in the report at £2,000,000. In September of the following year, 1868, the accompanying letter from the President of the Commission announced that the report had been favourably accepted :—

To JAMES ABERNETHY, Civil Engineer,
        2, Delahay Street, Westminster, London.

I have the honour to announce to you that His Majesty the Emperor on the 12th of this month graciously consented that the Danube, near Vienna, ought to be regulated after the line proposed by you and M. Sexauer.

With full respect,

SCHOLL,

Vienna, 18th September, 1868.   Major-General.

HUNGARY.

1866.

WHILE serving as a member of the Commission for the regulation of the similar Danube, he was further requested by his Excellency M. Mailath, Chancellor of Hungary, to inspect and report upon the regulation of the River Theiss, a large river which, flowing in a depressed bed through the centre of that country, acted as a drain in dry weather, depriving the land of moisture, but during periods of flood, owing to a deficiency of sectional area, causing extensive inundations in the districts of country near Pesth, and more especially further southwards, near the town of Szegedin. Accompanied by Major Ghyczy, an officer of the Imperial Engineers, who spoke English fluently, the two journeyed from Vienna to Buda, through the treeless plains inhabited by peasantry clad in sheepskin dresses and high jack boots, which enable them to wade through the deep mud in wet weather, the surface of the roads being for the most part alluvial soil, entirely destitute of stones or any hard materials. Even in the larger villages the inhabitants were chiefly of the same peasant class, the exceptions being government officials, doctors, and priests. Railway facilities were afforded to Pesth, Szegedin and Debreczin, but long distances were traversed in the small springless wagons of the country, from which the travellers alighted at nightfall to take up quarters at the post houses, which were almost exclusively in the hands of Jewish postmasters, who offered very indifferent food and viands, and sorry looking horses to further the journey in the day time. On one particular evening (Jan. 28th, 1896), difficulties overtook them by a collapse of the animal drawing the vehicle, in an out of the way district, and the discomfort of a night spent under the canopy of heaven seemed to be threatening as their lot, when they obtained the information that there was the château of a Hungarian gentleman close at hand. At that time, however, there was considerable estrangement between the Austrians and Hungarians, and Major Ghyczy being an Austrian officer, had considerable misgivings as to appealing to the hospitality of the owner of the château, but as the former could speak the Hungarian dialect the venture was made and with a successful issue. They were

kindly welcomed and partook of a good supper and
spent an enjoyable and interesting evening with their
host, while the engineer's limited command of French
enabled him to converse with the intelligent hostess.
Good horses were put at their disposal in the morning,
and accompanied by their host on horseback for several
miles, they proceeded to the isolated hill and village of
Tokay, by the River Theiss, which was reached in a
snowstorm, and quarters obtained at the house of a
government official. This gentleman was also a wine
producer, and provided some samples of the capability
of the vines in his district. Three days later they had
again got as far south as Szedegin, from which town
they returned to Pesth, staying at the Hotel Queen
Victoria. That town, like Vienna, was in a transitional
state, fine new streets and buildings in course of progress, which presented a striking contrast to the ancient
quarters of the Turk at the ancient city of Alt-ofen
or Buda on the right bank of the River Danube.
While staying at Pesth his diary records introductions
to several leading Hungarians, among others Counts
Bathyani and Schenzi, and a leading politician,
M. Deak.

The result of the visit to the region traversed by the
river Theiss, was in the cause of irrigation, the
recommendation of a new canal eighty miles in
length, from Löh to the river Koros, previously

advocated by M. Herrick, engineer, of Buda. Upon
returning to Vienna, General Baron Scholl escorted
the English representative on the commission to the
Island of Lobau, Napoleon the First's position previous
to his sudden appearance on the mainland on the
morning before the battle of Wagram on 6th July,
1809, in which he defeated the Archduke Charles.
Before leaving the city of Vienna, the members of the
commission were entertained by some of the city
authorities in the old Town Hall, which contained
many relics of the Turkish army of 200,000 men, under
the command of the Grand Vizier, Kara Mustapha,
defeated and driven from the walls by the Duke of
Lorraine and John Sobieski in 1683.

A friendship of a more lasting character was made
at this time with Field-Marshal Baron Jochmus, a
remarkably handsome man and of great stature.
When resident in London he occasionally came to dine
at 11, Prince of Wales Terrace, Kensington. Baron
Scholl, too, was a frequent guest there, between the
years 1866—8, and occasionally English officers were
invited to meet them, among others the author can
re-call Colonel Jervois R.E., now Sir William Jervois,
K.C.B.

EGYPT

Alexandria 1867-8.

E ARLY in the year 1867, the Khedive of Egypt, Ismail Pacha, visited England, and during his stay in London requested the late Mr. J. R. Maclean, M.P., C.E., and Mr. Abernethy, through his Minister, Nubar Pacha, to design works for the improvement of the harbour of Alexandria. Accordingly, accompanied by the Secretary of the Institution of Civil Engineers, the late Mr. Charles Manby, the engineers left England on the 5th February, and travelling *viâ* Brindisi, reached Alexandria on the evening of the 10th. A fortnight later upon their return to London they advocated to His Highness a scheme of which the chief recommendations were the construction of a breakwater from Eunostos Point to protect the harbour from westerly winds, the building of quays in

front of the city, provision for additional railway facilities
for the export and import trades, and lastly, a shorter
overland route to Suez. The report was duly submitted to His Highness, and the engineers were requested to attend on the 16th of July, at Lord Dudley's
house, in Park Lane, where they were presented to
the Khedive. His Highness expressed approval of the
scheme submitted by them, except as to certain proffered
railway facilities direct with the palace, by which, if
carried out, the members of the household and harem
would have been enabled to enter the train without
driving through the city to the existing station.
After several subsequent interviews with Nubar Pasha,
in Paris, during the summer, a second invitation to
visit Egypt was received and accepted in the month
of December. On this occasion they were joined by
the late Sir George Elliot, Bart., M.P., and Professor
Owen, and the entire party celebrated Christmas
Day, 1867, in the kitchen of Shepheard's Hotel,
whither they had repaired in order to be near a fire,
with songs, etc., the genial professor being one of
the merriest. The late Sir Samuel Baker was also a
guest at the hotel at this time, busying himself with
preparations for the expected visit of H.R H. The Prince
of Wales. At Cairo, several further interviews took
place both with the Khedive and his Minister of Public
Works, at some of which Colonel Staunton, Her

Majesty's Consul was present, but nothing more definite
than an expression of general approval of the project
ever resulted.   The delay was difficult to account for,
especially as the requisite capital was forthcoming, but
subsequently it was reported to have been due to the
influence of some eminent French engineers who were
held in high esteem by the Egyptian Government at
the time, and who presumably were somewhat jealous
of English intervention on Egyptian soil.

The various interviews were conducted amid a strong
seasoning of tobacco, and, occasionally with an in-
difference to time and attention to the topic under
discussion, which, although wholly unsatisfactory from
a business point of view, left a certain charm on the
memory as having constituted a novel experience.
During one such interview with a certain Minister, by
way of illustration, a small packet was brought in and
handed to His Excellency, who immediately proceeded
to open and read it slowly from beginning to end
several times, which occupied so much of the portion
of the afternoon available for further discussion con-
cerning the proposed harbour works, that it was thought
desirable to postpone proceedings till another day, and
this was accordingly done.   The missive, it subsequently transpired was nothing more important than a
play bill of a French theatrical company who were
to perform in the evening at the Khedive's Palace.

While passing the Christmas at Cairo, the English Government instructed Mr. Abernethy to visit and report upon the construction of a temporary hospital for invalid soldiers during the forthcoming Abyssinian Expedition, numbers of whom were already encamped near Suez, at that time little more than an Arab village, with a highly disreputable population. The house of the English Consul, Mr. Green, and the Peninsular and Oriental Hotel being the two more imposing buildings, and constituting two very agreeable exceptions to the rest. Having visited the hospital upon one occasion and dined with some officers at the hotel, he left later in the evening on the return journey to Cairo by a "special" train, consisting of an engine and tender and one dilapidated first-class carriage, of which he was the sole occupant. All went well till early in the morning, when he was suddenly pitched off the seat on to the floor, and a few seconds later the train was brought to a standstill. On alighting, his momentary apprehension of the engine and carriage having left the metals was at once confirmed, and it was equally obvious that there they must remain till some assistance in the form of a break-down gang arrived on the scene. The driver and guard, who were both Bedouins, and wholly unacquainted with either the English or French languages, soon showed what they considered the best thing to do under the circumstances, by wrapping themselves up in their *bournouses* and making preparations to sleep on the sand, while the passenger returned to the "special" and followed their example. This last selection, however, was the less safe of the two, for in addition to the possible danger of collision, the compartment contained among its musty cushions a scorpion, and the insect happening to awake while the passenger still slept, took the opportunity of inflicting a severe sting on the back of the sleeper's right hand. At first he thought it was the bite of some large fly and paid little attention to the painful wound, but the swelling of the entire arm which shortly afterwards ensued, suggested that it might have serious consequences. Leaving the carriage to arouse the driver and guard, he saw in the distance the smoke of a train approaching from Suez, and thus had sufficient time to walk down the line for some distance to meet it, and signal to the driver to stop The signal was understood, and the train, filled with homeward-bound English passengers, safely stopped, and with the assistance of the newly arrived officials and passengers, the way was cleared, and the journey to Cairo resumed—the two Arabs and the "special" being left to shift for themselves. Upon arrival at Cairo an English doctor at once applied poultices, etc,, and these were continued for several days, but the poisonous effect of the sting deprived him

of the use of his right arm for some weeks afterwards.

It was during the first visit to Egypt, in February,
1867, that he first made the acquaintance of M.,
afterwards Count de Lesseps, to whom he was introduced, as his diary records, on March 17th, by Mr.
Laing, the English representative on the Suez Canal
Board, who remarked to M. de Lesseps that the English
engineer he was introducing was one of those who
scouted the opinion held by some members of the
profession that the making of the Suez Canal was
impracticable. M. de Lesseps after some further conversation, invited him to stay at his house for a week,
and during this time he paid visits to the Canal Works,
then in active progress, with his host. He also accompanied Monsieurs Voisin and Laroche to Suez,
where he stayed at the house of the former, and rode
by stages on horseback to Port Said, where he was the
guest of M. Laroche.

Ismailia, at this time, where the chief engineer resided, presented a French aspect with its newly-formed
boulevards planted on either side. In the centre of the
courtyard, adjoining his house, was a bath supplied
with water from the adjoining, or what was termed,
the Sweet Water Canal, and from the window of the
bedroom facing this courtyard, the guest was much
amused, while dressing one morning at seeing his good

L

host seated up to his neck in the bath, with several of his staff round him reading papers and conversing with them. Writing of the distinguished French engineer, who accompanied him on the greater part of a ride from Suez to Port Said, he stated—" I have never met his equal: although sixty years old he is an accomplished horseman, and active beyond the majority of young and even athletic men; " and of the work of making the Suez Canal, upon which he was engaged, that he was "Carrying it out, with the assistance of able engineers, whose talents from the simple character of the work they are engaged on, are confined to organization as to the best and most economical methods of excavation and dredging, and in this his contractor, Lavallay, displays much energy."

In the summer of the year 1871, the work at the harbour of Alexandria was commenced by a company of contractors who were also their own engineers— Messrs. Greenfield & Co. This being an arrangement inconsistent with Mr. Abernethy's experience hitherto as a Civil Engineer, he declined to act in the twofold capacity, as one of the partners in the firm, and engineer to the same, and as the Egyptian Government insisted upon the scheme being carried out on different lines to what he had designed, and apparently with no improvement, his connection with the undertaking ceased. The foundation stone was laid by the Khedive, on May

15th, 1871, with great ceremony, and the work completed in 1874, but the plan of 1867 was considerably
modified, and that the modification proved in the end
to have detracted from the value of the original designs,
the Official Report of Alexandria, written by Her
Majesty's Consul, Mr. Stanley, in July, 1874, expressly
affirms in these words,—

"The harbour works at Alexandria are approaching
completion. The great breakwater will be finished in
a month, and the inner mole run out to within a short
distance of its entire length of 980 yards. The
direction of the mole has been changed since 1871,
when I sent a plan of it which was published with my
report of that year. It now runs out straight to the
lighthouse, whereas before, after running in this direction 200 yards, it was to make a bend to the arsenal.
This it was found would cramp the harbour, so the
direction has been changed. The portion already
begun, has been completed, and will form an arm of
the main mole. The mole is intended to be upwards
of 100 feet broad. Vessels are not to come alongside
it, but small iron jetties will run out for them. The
quays, which are to be formed from the railway to the
Custom House, have not been begun. It has been
found necessary to abandon the idea of having perpen-
dicular quay walls, alongside of which vessels could
lie, owing to the great difficulty of getting a proper

L 2

foundation, there being 40 feet of mud, so they will be roughly formed of rubble and stone, and iron piers will be run out at intervals.

"It will be seen that the original plan has been much modified. It seems also generally allowed that Mr. Abernethy's plan for the breakwater was infinitely better than the one adopted by the Egyptian Government. His plan was to run out the breakwater on the inner bank of the shoal. The consequence of its being on the outer bank is that there is a distance of nearly a mile between it and the shipping, so that with a strong wind there is room for a sufficiently heavy sea to get up to prevent working. Had the breakwater been run out on the inner shoal, the harbour would have been practically as large as at present, the intervening space being too shallow and rocky for vessels to anchor in, and shipping work could have been carried on in all weathers."

LAKE ABOUKIR.

1887-8.

AFTER an interval of nearly twenty years since his visit to Alexandria, Mr. Abernethy designed a scheme for the reclamation of Lake Aboukir, and acted as consulting engineer during the execution of the work to an English Company, which had obtained a concession from the Egyptian Government through the instrumentality of Mr. William Grant to effect that object. While Mr. H. G. Sheppard, Assoc. M. Inst. C.E., undertook the position of resident engineer at the scene of operations.

Lake Aboukir was distant but six miles from the city of Alexandria, and constituted one of a series of salt lakes along the northern coast, between that city and Port Said. Its area, as defined in the concession of March 12th, 1887, was 29,621 feddans, or 30,717

acres (1 feddan = 1·037 acre).   In section it was shaped
like a saucer, flat in the centre and rising towards the
edges, while the average level of the centre was about
3·28 feet below mean sea level.   None of the land, even
around the edges, was sufficiently high to admit of
draining the water into the sea, which was excluded by
a stone sea wall.

The bed of the lake, like those of the rest of the
lakes in the district, being some feet below the level of
the sea, could only be drained by means of pumping
and discharging the water into the sea, which entails
a heavy charge on lands reclaimed, or by means of siphons
or culverts under the Mahmoudieh Canal, running off
the water into Lake Mareotis, the mean level of the
water in the latter lake being about 4·92 feet below
the bed of Lake Aboukir.

The latter naturally commended itself as being the
cheaper and more efficient plan, but, unfortunately,
it failed to meet with the approval of the Egyptian
Ministry, and the system of pumping was specified as a
sine quâ non in the concession.

Even reclamation by the system of pumping was,
however, considered to be a profitable undertaking from
the facts of the lake being situated on the outskirts of a
rapidly growing city of 250,000 inhabitants, with two
railways and a large canal encircling three sides, and
the annual rent of land in the vicinity being £5 per acre.

From the month of May to August in each year—
the period of the hot season—the lake used to be completely dry before the work of reclamation was begun,
but during the high Nile and winter months was covered
with water to about nine inches in depth over the bed,
and there the water would remain till evaporated in
the following summer.

This water was partly rain water and partly drainage
water from the cultivated lands, but there was little or
no infiltration from the sea. From this it will be
gathered that the lake was clearly a large salt-evapo-
rating basin—the salt being almost pure chloride of
sodium—the sale of which was a Government mon-
opoly. Each year this deposit of salt, probably
increasing in quantity, was alternately dissolved by
the winter rains and dried by the summer heat, and
this, and this alone, prevented the successful cultivation of the bed of the lake.

The presence of the salt some three or four inches
thick in the depressions of the bed of the lake is
accounted for in various ways. Firstly, it is inherent
in the whole of the deltaic formation of Lower Egypt,
while it is also stated that during a great storm in the
year 1715 the sea wall was breached by the sea, and
that for years after the breach remained open. Possibly
also the sea being at a higher level than the lake would
tend to force any salts to the surface, even if the salt

water itself could not penetrate to an appreciable extent.

The site of the lake was cultivated and populated in the days of the Pharoahs, as the buried remains of ancient towns scattered over its surface made manifest.

The method of reclamation adopted was by a complete system of drainage and fresh-water canals, which derived their supply from the Mahmoudieh Canal, which bounded it on the west and south. But the work of reclaiming the lake was of a more interesting character than the mere pumping out of its water, for it included also the deposition upon the land of a layer of rich alluvial matter held in suspension in the waters of the Nile. In fact the irrigation was even of more importance than the drainage. While the admission of the Nile water, admitted and allowed to remain for a certain period, absorbed the salt in the soil, it at the same time deposited the soil held in solution, which, after the water had been pumped, became sweetened, and the clear water was run off into drains, which conducted it to the pumps erected on the line of railway to Rosetta, within 350 metres (383 yards) of the sea.

The engines and pumps of immense power, supplied by Messrs. J. & H. Gwynne & Co., of London, commenced working on March 8th, 1888, and on April 23rd a telegram was received, announcing that Lake Aboukir was dry, the water having been pumped off in the short space of 45 days, with a consumption of but 135 tons of coal.   To state the net result in figures, 2,900,000,000 gallons of water were lifted to an average height of six feet, with the consumption of fuel above-mentioned: equal to raising 21½ million gallons six feet high per ton of coal, or 9,600 gallons of salt water the same height for each pound of coal used : in other words, one pound of coal sufficed to raise 96,000 pounds of water six feet.

The process of flooding and pumping out the lake was repeated several times, and ultimately the soil was rendered fertile.   Steam ploughs were soon busy at work, and the Egyptian Lakes Reclamation Company had numerous applications for leases of portions of the area reclaimed, which in 1890 was described as " a waving sea of green crop "—Wineba being presumably the green crop alluded to.

THE CHANNEL FERRY.

1870-2.

THE troubles and miseries of a passage in the small and stuffy boats across that short but uncomfortable strip of seas, known as the Straits of Dover or Pas de Calais, had so far successfully aggravated the feelings of the daily and nightly victims of business or pleasure who traversed to and fro in the year 1870, that there arose what might be termed a general outcry for something better. "Rude waves" far too frequently, irrespective of age, infancy, or sex, dashed over the unfortunate passengers on such boats as "the *Petrel*, the *Wave*, and the *Foam*," who shunned the proffered saloon accommodation below, preferring what rough shelter they could find on deck. One writer to the papers at this date, possibly an American, gives expression to his feelings by saying, "The way in which that passage across a strip of water is conducted in these days of incessant international communication, is one of the wonders of the age." On clear days the opposite coast of France loomed clearly and hospitably to the eye, but the problem as to how the horrors that lay between were to be lessened or overcome, remained and still remains unsolved.

The traveller descending from the train upon its arrival at the Admiralty Pier at Dover stills feels only too frequently :—

> " Like one that stands upon a promontory,
> And spies a far off shore where he would tread,
> Wishing his foot were equal with his eye ;
> And chides the sea that sunders him from thence,
> Saying, he'll lade it dry to have his way."
>
> 3rd Part King Henry VI., Act 3, s. 2.

The sight of the cliffs of two great and wealthy nations but seven leagues distant from each other has long since suggested to the people of both various schemes of different degrees of practicability, but all of them probably more practical in their conception, and feasable of execution than that suggested by the quotation. There have been the submerged tube lying on the bottom, the submarine shield, the bridge of M. Charles Boutet, the tunnel, first advocated by M. de Gamond in 1838, and the ferry plying between piers. But it is the latter scheme only, put forward by Messrs. Fowler and Abernethy that need be, and the only one probably

that should be described in this biography. The re-
quirement of larger boats and of greater power which
would make the passage quickly and give plenty of
room and comfort to the passengers, in place of the
existing packets, was widely recognised, and to the
many who were of opinion that the other schemes
aimed at too much, and were convinced that the then
existing service with the Continent aimed at too little,
the Channel Ferry scheme found favour as a happy
medium. But the dimensions of the packets have to
be determined by the exigencies of trade and harbours.
Calais and Boulogne were ports so small that only
small steamers could enter, and Dover was not much
better. Here was the foundation of the difficulty.
Packets of greatly increased size could not run into
the ports on the French coast, even if they could at
Dover, and so before the boats could be enlarged,
the ports required to be first enlarged to receive them.
Much bigger boats were considered as the first essential, but before that first essential, came the necessity
for larger harbours to receive them.

It was in 1870 that Mr. (now Sir) John Fowler and
Mr. Abernethy brought forward their scheme for a new
International Communication between England and
France. They suggested in the first place further
protection and accommodation at Dover by lengthening
the Admiralty Pier 300 feet, and constructing a second

pier or breakwater, projecting from the southern end of the Marine Parade for a distance of 400 feet in a south-easterly direction, so as to ensure a large enclosure of smooth water in which the proposed steam ferry boats, which will be referred to shortly, would find a harbour in any weather and at any state of the tide, while a huge water-shed was to be erected with a glass roof into which both train and boat were to run, and these works would have had the further effect of rendering the harbour a harbour of shelter to vessels running in from stress of weather. The necessity of improving Calais or Boulogne Harbour simultaneously with Dover involved the consent and co-operation of the French Government, all harbours in France being under direct State control, but the French Government were much in favour of the project, the Emperor Napoleon III. especially so, and the improvement of the selected port on the French coast was to be entrusted to French engineers. No little diplomacy was required, however, in successfully representing the scheme to the French Government, and the two English engineers who brought it forward, and made themselves professionally responsible for its design, were several times summoned to Paris between the years 1869 and 1872. In December, 1869, the late Right Hon. Ward Hunt, then First Lord of the Admiralty, who took much interest in the proposed scheme, accompanied by the

two engineers, had a long interview by appointment
with the Emperor at the Tuileries.

Ushered by an aide-de-camp through several apartments, the visitors found the Emperor in a small room,
wearing a plain brown tweed suit and devoid of
anything in the way of Orders. He at once rose to
meet them as they entered, shook hands heartily,
and requested his English guests to be seated at a small
table with him. He listened to the proposed scheme
with great interest, and after it had been represented
to him, expressed his desire to do all in his power to
support it. He also stated that to the best of his
recollection a somewhat similar project had been submitted to him some time back, and rang for his
secretary, to whom upon his appearance he gave
instructions to search for the papers referring to it in
the adjoining library. After some time the secretary
returned and stated that he was unable to find them.
" Then I will try myself," said his majesty, and returned
after a short interval with his hands soiled with dust,
but without having found what he wanted.

The chief features in the proposed channel communication were these : The ferry boat, of 5000
tons burden, measuring 450 feet in length, 57 feet beam,
and 95 feet over the paddle-boxes, with a draught of
12ft. 6in., a foot less draught than the Dublin and
Holyhead boats of that time, and with engines of 1400

horse power, capable of giving a speed of 20 knots an
hour, and driven by four independent oscillating cylinder
engines, was to await the arrival of the trains in the
large water-shed under cover of a glass roof. The
trains of the South-Eastern and London Chatham
and Dover Companies were to be joined together
at Dover, and run direct on to the ferry boat. A great
feature in the scheme, was the method proposed of
taking the train on board by hydraulic lifts and raising
it to the requisite level, and Mr. Abernethy thus
described the process in his evidence before the Committee of the House of Lords :—" The railway carriages
will pass from the level of the rails on to the hydraulic
lift, and according to the state of the tide, the lift
will be lowered to any required level to enable the
carriages to be passed directly on to the midship
deck of the steamer. The lift itself will always
be on the level, and will be lowered to any requisite
extent by hydraulic power." Sir William (now Lord)
Armstrong calculated that the time occupied in putting
the passenger trains on the upper-deck would be five
minutes. It was estimated that 12 coaches on the
upper-deck, with the means of placing either 12
goods trucks or 8 additional coaches on the lower-
deck, which would then accommodate 288 passengers,
would be sufficient, and either could be done in five
minutes.

The idea of being able to take a seat in a railway
carriage in London, and not leaving it save by choice,
until arrival eight hours later in Paris, found favour
with a large section of the public, while the offered
facility of despatching a railway truck full of goods
direct from London to Berlin or Vienna, *without breaking bulk*, appealed forcibly to merchants and to the
railway companies. The train once on board, a
passenger could open his carriage door, betake himself
as he felt disposed (or indisposed), to a private cabin
at its side, walk to a handsome refreshment room,
or mount to the outer deck, (for the train occupied the
centre of the deck saloon, exactly as a dinner table does
in ordinary steamers.)

The train would thus pass from London to Paris as
unbrokenly as from London to Dover, the only difference
being in the motive power while crossing the Straits,
and on arrival, the bow or the stern of the boat would
be again opened in the same manner as lock-gates, the
hydraulic lift lowered to the requisite level to receive
the train, raise it to the level of the permanent
way, and the journey to Paris could then be continued.
As a further convenience to passengers, in addition to
not having to change carriages, with the sole result of
exchanging one seat for another exactly similar, all the
incidental trouble of looking after luggage would be
avoided, and to secure despatch, it was intended

that the luggage should be searched during the passage.

The proposed powerful boats were obviously intended to save time, and in those days, when the average passage was about one hour and three-quarters, they would certainly have fulfilled the object of their design. There would as certainly have been a saving of temper with respect to the luggage. Safety in bad weather was a second feature in the design of these monster ferry-boats, and as a corollary to their hugeness, it was confidently anticipated by many, both experts and non-experts in seamanship, that sea-sickness would be reduced to a minimum by the steadiness with which they would travel. Many were to be found, no doubt, who took this assurance *cum grano salis*, for there are many people who exhibit almost a pre-disposition to be ill as soon as they step on board, and make preparations for their coming misery before the steamer is under weigh. The late Sir Luke Smithett, who was engaged in the service between Dover and Calais for thirty years, in his evidence before Parliament, offered hope even to such as these. "There would," said he, "be much less motion in these boats, and consequently much less sea-sickness. There would be no pitching, and, if they went at the speed proposed, they would not have time to roll."

The harbour of Calais, however, not being considered

M

capable of the required improvement for this traffic, a
site for a new deep water harbour was selected at
Andresselles, a little to the south of Cape Grisnez,
which was thought to possess considerable natural
facilities, and had been well reported upon by French
engineers to their Government. While on a certain
visit early in the year 1872 to this spot, he met his old
friend Mr. George Hudson, the deposed railway king,
for whom he ever entertained feelings of respect, and
whom, though he had fallen from his high estate
into one of poverty, he continued to regard as an unfortunate catspaw of others, who better deserved to be
in his then reduced circumstances. Mr. Hudson,
whom he met at the railway station on the arrival of
the boat at Calais, joined him, by invitation, at dinner
that evening, at Dessien's Hotel, and during the dinner,
gave a graphic description of his fêtes at Albert Gate,
and of the many who toadied to him, with a view to
their own advantage, and their very different behaviour
when misfortunes began to overtake him.

The Bill passed in 1870, but was withdrawn in
consequence of the Franco-German War, and on its
renewal in 1872, it was unexpectedly thrown out by a
Committee of the House of Lords, presided over by
the late Lord Lawrence, ex-Governor-General of India.

The cost of the works on this side of the Channel
was put down in the Parliamentary estimate at

£890,000, and the time within which the works would be completed, three years. With the rejection of the Channel Ferry scheme by the House of Lords, attention was diverted again to the proposed tunnel, advocated by Sir James Brunlees, and at length authorized and commenced by a company, of which Sir Edward Watkin, was chairman. With the subsequent history of this gigantic work, its stoppage, abandonment, and utilization of the site of the approach to the Tunnel as an approach to the Kent coal fields, all readers are familiar. None of the rival schemes have been carried out. The railway companies' new boats have no doubt vastly improved the service in recent years, and there is no longer the same occasion for complaining of the service. Great improvements have been effected at Dover, Calais, and Boulogne harbours, but the remarks in Mr. Abernethy's presidential address to the Institute of Civil Engineers in 1881,—eleven years after the rejection of the Channel Ferry scheme—were true when spoken, "at Dover the single pier affords no adequate shelter during on shore gales; the entrance to the harbour and the anchorage are entirely unprotected. On the French coast, at the nearest point to our own, nature has provided great facilities for the construction of a deep water harbour, but local interests have hitherto prevailed over national interests, and nothing effective has yet been done, nor is there much promise

M 2

in the immediate future. The entrance to Calais harbour is, if anything, in a worse condition than it was in past years, and the problem of forming a deep water harbour at Boulogne, on an extensive range of sandy foreshore, by enclosing a large space with backwater, remains to be solved." The large scheme now being carried out by the Government will far more than embody the proposals of 1870, as regards improving and sheltering the harbour.

NEWPORT (MON.)

1856-1885.

UNTIL the year 1834 the splendid river Usk, upon the banks of which Newport is situated, alone supplied the necessary conveniences for the commerce of the port, but by that date the trade with foreign ports carried on in vessels of large tonnage, had increased to such an extent, that it was deemed advisable to provide floating dock accommodation. A company accordingly, was formed for that purpose, and an Act obtained in 1835 to construct a basin and lock communicating with the river, which was duly finished and opened for traffic in 1842, at an expenditure of £195,000. This floating basin covered an area of four acres, and the lock through which it was entered, 220 feet by 61 feet, was considered one of the finest in the kingdom.

In 1854 the company obtained a further Act, em-
powering them to convert the feeder pond into a floating
dock, and so add another seven-and-a-half acres to the
existing floating area, thereby making a total of eleven-
and-a-half acres.   For the execution of this work they
engaged the professional services of Mr. Abernethy,
and the work was completed and opened in March,
1858.   The coal trade carried on at these docks, (where
coal hoists were worked by hydraulic machinery
furnished by Sir W. G. Armstrong and Co.) soon became
so extensive, and continued to increase so rapidly, that
much overcrowding and consequent delay in loading
was experienced—the returns for the year 1864 showing
a shipment of 322,646 tons of coal, or 28,913 tons to
each acre of dock area.

The effect of the large shipment of steam coal, moreover, was to reduce the number of sailing vessels and
attract a larger proportion of steamers for the export
trade, by which change, increased despatch and regularity of journey were secured.   In addition to this,
many of the steamers frequenting the port exceeded
300 feet in length, so that more accommodation, as well
as the best modern appliances for loading and despatching them in the shortest possible time, became impera-
tive for the welfare of Newport, as a competing port in
the Bristol Channel.   To secure the last object large
additional space for sidings and storage was requisite,

so that the coal might be standing in readiness
to be shipped as soon as the steamers arrived, and these
facilities were not obtainable in the vicinity of the
existing docks. The inadequate accommodation to
meet the demands of trade had in fact not only become
realized, but actual falling off in traffic had set in, and
was threatening to still further increase for the coal
and iron merchants in the district gladly encouraged
every attempt that was made to obtain direct railway
communication between their various works and the
Port of Cardiff, where, including Penarth and the area
inside the old Canal Gates to the Great Western
Railway Bridge, there was still-water accommodation
of 94 acres.

Such is an epitome of affairs at Newport, when a
new company, of which the late Lord Tredegar was
chairman, was formed in 1864, and application made
to Parliament for powers to make the Alexandra Docks ;
Mr. Abernethy, who had acted for the old company in
1856-8, being again entrusted with the engineering,
and deputed to prepare the Parliamentary plans and
sections, and subsequently all the detailed drawings.

The project met with the unanimous support of all
the railway companies in the district, but a moiety of
the directors in the old company, apprehensive of an
injury to the trade in their dock, opposed it, and
tendered evidence before Parliament to the effect that

the then existing dock was amply sufficient for the trade, that no further space would be required for years to come, and that they could, if necessary, ship double the quantity of coal at present sent down for exportation.

With this evidence to contend against, the promoters of the Alexandra Dock experienced a severe struggle before the Committees of both Houses of Parliament, but they succeeded in obtaining their Act, to which the royal assent was given on July 6th, 1865.

When the work was authorized and about to be commenced trade was flourishing, and with a certain stability which induced a firm hope that it would continue. The "black diamonds," the produce of the district, were sought for and supplied with a will. But while the company were indulging in sanguine expectations of the speedy commencement of the great undertaking fraught with such prospective advantages, the sudden collapse of the great house of Overend, Gurney & Co., followed by an almost unparalleled panic, and a subsequent period of distrust and stagnation in the monetary and commercial world, necessitated the suspension of operations. Strikes between employer and employée, too, tended to drive trade from the district in common with others, while the crisis in the east paralysed speculators, and trade reached a low ebb indeed.

As soon, however, as there was a partial revival
of confidence, the promoters again pushed forward
their scheme with energy, and their efforts received
invaluable aid from the secretary, the late Mr. J. S.
Adam. By mutual agreement some changes were
effected in the directorate, a few gentlemen retiring
to allow of the admission of some enterprising capitalists,
notably the late Mr. J. R. McLean and Sir George
Elliot, in their stead, but continuing to support and
further the undertaking. After careful deliberation it
was decided to proceed with a portion of the original
scheme, and to do this on such a plan, that at any
time the entire work could be completed without
inconvenience and within the original estimated cost.

Accordingly on May 28th, 1868, the work was commenced, the ceremony of turning the first sod being
performed by Lady Tredegar, the engineer handing
her a silver spade for the occasion and remarking,—
"Your ladyship, I present to you this implement for
the inauguration of a great work, which I have no
doubt will prove a source of gratification to your
noble husband and his family in future years, conducing,
as it must, to the prosperity of the trade of Newport
and neighbourhood."

After seven years of unremitting patient work the
Alexandra Dock was completed, and on April 17th, 1875,
the mayor was in the fortunate position of being able

to telegraph to H.R.H the Prince of Wales, at Sandringham, that " The Alexandra Dock, named after H.R.H. the Princess of Wales, has just been opened in the presence of 40,000 people of all classes, amid the universal rejoicings of the inhabitants of Wales."

The latter words might, if subjected to strict criticism, be regarded as a gentle hit at the exclusion of Monmouthshire from the Principality of Wales, for which the adjusters of the Oxford Circuit were responsible, as it was aforetime inalienably Welsh, but probably there was a sufficient proportion of Welshmen among those present, and certainly more than a sufficient number throughout Wales who were not present, but who shared in the rejoicings, to make the message correct. His Royal Highness, in reply, took up the same strain, for he wired,—"I thank you much for your telegram, and I congratulate most heartily *the inhabitants of Wales* on the success of the undertaking."

The Alexandra Dock is situated about one mile from the mouth of the Usk, a broad and deep river, having a width of 700 feet opposite to the entrance of the dock, and a depth of 37 feet, and without a single obstacle of any kind to its navigability either by day or night. The land upon which it was constructed was the property of Lord Tredegar, the chairman of the Alexandra Dock Company, and ample space was

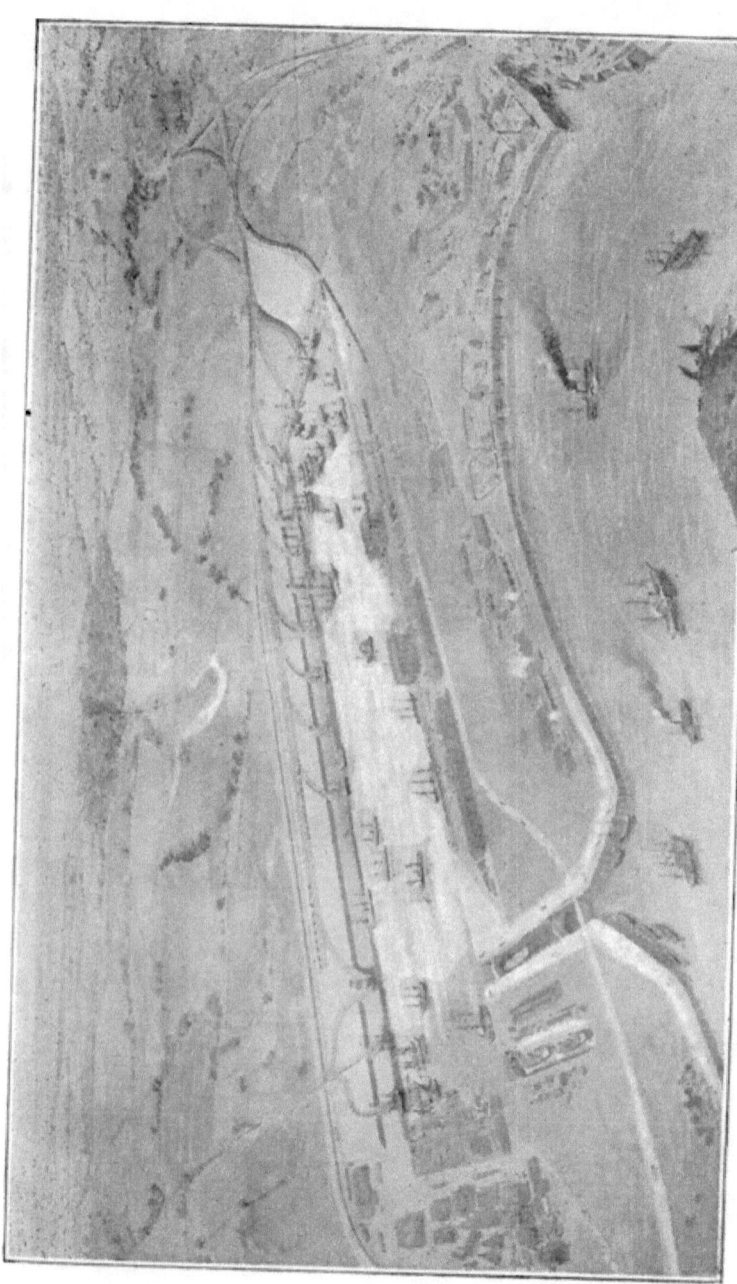

ALEXANDRA DOCK, NEWPORT, MONMOUTH, OPENED APRIL 17TH, 1875.

secured, capable of future extension, on which to make an elaborate labyrinth of sidings.

The entrance to the Alexandra Dock is admirably situated at a bend of the river Usk, and being in the design of a "trumpet mouth," affords the greatest facilities for working vessels in and out. The curves being common to both directions, enable vessels to be passed in beyond the tideway of the river at once without the necessity of swinging them across the channel as had to be done in entering the old dock. This "trumpet mouth" entrance is 350 feet wide between the line of the river front and the outer gates, with a depth of 37 feet of water on average spring tides.

The principal works comprise an outer lock 350 feet by 65 feet, divided by a pair of intermediate gates, so that it may be used as two locks, or one large lock as required, and vessels drawing 23 feet of water can enter or leave within an average period of three hours on every tide throughout the year. The Alexandra Dock, which receives its water supply from the river Ebbw by means of a conduit, has an area of 28¾ acres, and being in immediate connection with all the existing lines into Newport, secures the most complete through communication for import as well as for export traffic. The chief imports are Baltic and Norwegian timber, pit props, Spanish iron ore, and railway sleepers; and exports, in addition to coal, iron, machinery, sleepers, rails, and tin. The hydraulic coal hoists constructed by Messrs. Armstrong, Mitchell and Co., from designs supplied by Mr. Abernethy, are most efficient. These machines, which are of a high and low level are also ingenious in their method of work. The lift receives a truck full of coal from the low level metals, raises it to the shoot, tips its contents into the vessels hold, then lets the empty truck slip down the slightly inclined high level, along which it travels to join the empties.

After the opening of the Alexandra Docks many strides were made in the commercial progress of the port. Step by step the directors added to the facilities already given for the trade, and on August 7th, 1878, a large graving dock, 500 feet in length and 56 feet in width at the bottom, and 74 feet in width at the coping, was completed. The bottom is inverted, and has a verse line of one foot six inches. This graving dock is supplied by water from the dock, which in its turn is supplied by the river Ebbw, thereby avoiding the use of tidal water, which generally leaves a deposit of mud. The water is ultimately discharged into the river through a three feet cast-iron pipe, which is taken down to low-water mark. This arrangement further did away with the necessity of pumping, which docks supplied from a river, usually require. The last mentioned work was completed in thirteen months, to the great credit of the contractor, the late Mr. John Griffiths.

A large timber pond which had been in course of construction, simultaneously with the graving dock, was the next work executed, and later a staging and jetty were added for the shipment of rails. The timber pond constructed is 300 feet long and 100 feet wide, and is connected with the dock by a canal some 800 feet in length, through which the timber on arrival is passed into the float. The Alexandra Dock has been lengthened since 1875, under the direction of the late Sir George Elliot, Bart., plans for which were prepared for him by Mr. Abernethy in 1885.

CARDIFF.

1866-96.

THE commercial history of Cardiff begins with the present century, and its development is strictly contemporaneous with that of the mineral wealth of the county; archæologically it dates back to the first century, when Aulus Didius founded a Roman station at the mouth of the River Taff.

Situated at the end of the Taff valley, the town furnished the most accessible outlet for the products of the minerals in the hill districts to the northward, and it was further endowed with the great natural advantages of a roadstead, a harbour, and a river whence the minerals could be shipped. These given advantages, as well as the knowledge of the wealth lying hidden close at hand, became fully realized towards the close of the eighteenth century, and next year,

1898, will mark the centenary of the first serious attempt to open up the produce of the surrounding country, for it was in 1798 that the Glamorganshire Canal from Merthyr Tydvil to Cardiff, 25 miles distant, at which point it was connected with the Bristol Channel by a sea-lock, was completed and opened.

So great was the increase of traffic following the opening of the canal that thirty-three years later it was found necessary to make the first of the Bute Docks, and the Marquis of Bute applied for advice to some of the leading engineers and nautical experts of that day, Mr. Telford, Mr. Green, and Sir William Cubitt, Captains Beaufort and W. H. Smyth, R.N., the latter being subsequently entrusted with the chief direction of the work, and upon its completion obtaining the post of Dockmaster at the Bute West Dock. Twelve years later a second dock was found necessary to accommodate the traffic, and on this occasion, Sir John Rennie was engaged in conjunction with Mr. W. S. Clarke, who designed the Bute East Dock, the contractors for carrying out the work being Messrs. Hemmingway and Pearson.

In 1866, when the present marquis had succeeded to the title, the trustees who then acted for his lordship under the late marquis's will, applied for an Act to construct the Roath Basin, and on this occasion they first sought and enlisted Mr. Abernethy's services as

consulting engineer to prepare the parliamentary plans.
This Roath Basin of 12 acres became in its turn in-
sufficient for the requirements of the port, and in 1882,
together with the late Mr. McConnochie, C.E., he prepared new designs for the Roath Dock, which was opened
on August 24th, 1887, by the Marquis of Bute. This
fine dock has an area of 33 acres, and is upwards of
2,400 feet long and 600 feet wide, and the depth of
water varies from 36 feet to 25 feet, according to the
tide. It is entirely enclosed with walls of masonry,
thus affording the largest practicable extent of quayage,
as well as the greatest facilities for loading and discharging vessels. The length of quay space, including
the jetty, is 7520 lineal feet, or nearly 1½ mile, while
the area for the storage of cargoes and the
general carrying on of the trade of the dock is over
60 acres, and its capacity as a dock is equal to 5,000,000
tons per annum. It is approached through the Roath
Basin by a magnificent lock—the largest in the world
—600 feet by 80 feet, with a depth over the sills of
36 feet at ordinary spring tides and 26 feet at neaps.
The moveable hydraulic cranes by which the coal is
shipped with the least possible breakage, and which by
being moveable on rails obviates the necessity of shifting the vessel from its berth, or from hatchway to
hatchway, while loading, are the invention of Sir W. T.
Lewis, Bart., general manager of the Bute estates,

and are most efficient both in the saving of time and in the lessened labour of trimming the coal when shot into the vessel.

The increase in tonnage and carrying capacity of steamers plying to Cardiff for coal a few years later, called for additional, and even better, accommodation than that already found there, and in 1894 the Bute Dock Company, who had, by an Act obtained in 1888, secured sufficient additional foreshore to construct a new dock within the limits authorized, again successfully applied to Parliament for power to effect the work. Mr. Abernethy, in conjunction with Mr. Hunter, the Engineer to the Bute Docks Company, designed and submitted the scheme. The requisite area has been reclaimed by an embankment since obtaining the Act in 1894, and the actual work is now on the point of being begun in earnest, and is upon a scale which should meet the requirements of the port for many years to come.

The entrance lock will be 750 feet by 90 feet, and will be approached by an Outer Tidal Basin, recessed clear of the navigable channel leading to the existing dock entrances so as not to interfere with the shipping passing to and fro, and there will be a depth of 41 feet 6 inches over the sill at high water ordinary spring tides, and 31 feet 6 inches at high water ordinary neap tides.

N

The dock itself will have an area of 42 acres,
2570 feet in length and 650 feet in width, the depth
being 46 feet 8 inches below the coping, and with a
varying water depth of 37 feet to 32 feet. Between
this new dock and the Roath Dock there will be a
communication passage 300 feet wide for the first 700
feet of its length, and 80 feet wide for the remainder of
its junction with the Roath Dock. By means of this
passage large steamers will be able to pass to the new
deep entrance lock and thence seaward. At present,
owing to the defective size of the Roath Basin Lock,
passing the larger steamers in and out involves
levelling down the water in the Roath Basin itself,
and consequently a serious waste of water, as well as
loss of time. The Parliamentary estimate for this new
dock accommodation was £585,717; for the embankment, £42,935, and for the railways and sidings,
£8291, making a total of £636,944.

BELGIUM.

1880-81.

TEN years after the rejection of the Channel Ferry scheme between Dover and Cape Grisnez by the Committee of the House of Lords, presided over by Lord Lawrence, at the instigation of the South Eastern Railway Company, and accompanied by the Chairman, Sir Edward Watkin, M.P., and Sir Myles Fenton, General Manager, Mr. Abernethy visited Belgium, with a view to determining the advisability of improving the harbour either at Nieuport or Ostend, and to render one or the other accessible at all periods of the tide to the mail packets, and so establishing a regular service of inter-communication viâ Belgium between England and the Continent. Five years previously he had, in conjunction with the late Mr. Thomas Hawkesley, F.R.S., Past Pres. Inst. C.E., and Captain Calver, R.N., F.R.S., reported to his majesty in favour of improving the former port, chiefly in consequence of the natural advantages it possessed in having a far more extensive roadstead, and a larger area of deep water, than the port of Ostend. The predominance of opinion, however, in 1880, was in favour of improving the latter port, and several interviews took place with his majesty the King, or his Minister of Public Works, at which the project was discussed, and on March 7th, 1881, the English engineer reported against the system of improvement hitherto attempted at Ostend by sluicing from reservoirs at the periods of low water, in the following words:—

"The utter failure of attempting to maintain deep water harbours on sandy coasts by the creation of artificial reservoirs and sluicing, without the aid of dredging, is fully exemplified in the present condition of the harbours of Boulogne, Calais, and Ostend.

"In England, as far back as 1852, it was supposed that by constructing works for giving great effect to the outgoing currents, rivers such as the Tyne, Clyde, and others, would be deepened and maintained, and that the bars of sand at their entrances, as instanced in the case of the Tyne, composed of light sand, would be removed, but no such result followed, and it was only by resorting to dredging, and actually removing altogether the bar and banks within the channel of that

river to the extent of 62 million tons, that the present
satisfactory results have been attained. The bar, which
I sounded in 1850, and found but 6 feet upon it at
low water spring tides, has now at the same period of
the tide, a permanent depth of 20 feet, and the river
throughout its whole course to Newcastle Bridge, a
distance of 12 miles, is proportionally deepened, so that
at the highest point at Newcastle where the depth was
5 to 6 feet at low water in 1850, the present depth is
20 feet.

" Similar results by dredging have been effected at
the river Tees, and other rivers where extensive sandy
foreshores exist, and it must be borne in mind that in
these cases there are continuous outgoing currents
infinitely superior in force to the discharge from artificial reservoirs, such as those existing at Boulogne,
Calais, Ostend, and other ports.

" I am of opinion that the question of attempting to
maintain deep or low water harbours in the case of the
section of coast extending from Boulogne to the northern
extremity of the Belgian coast, is fully settled and
determined by the existing state of the harbours on
that coast.

" As far back as March, 1872, at the Chamber of
Commerce at Boulogne, in a discussion relative to the
formation of a deep water harbour there for a large
class of vessels, I expressed a strong opinion that it

was utterly futile to attempt the construction of such a harbour to be maintained by the sluicing power that then existed, which was and is very considerable, from the large area of the Bassin de Retenue at its head, together with the powerful sluicing apparatus in connection with it, and the present condition of the harbour, I think, fully corroborates the soundness of these views.

"As regards Calais, its condition is at the present time such that the small class of mail packets frequenting it cannot often enter at low water, and the regularity of the mail service is much disarranged, and I am informed that the authorities are now about to resort to extensive dredging operations.

"In the case of Ostend, the effect of sluicing the detritus from the inner portion of the harbour, as in all parallel cases, results in its deposition and the formation of banks at the entrance, which would not be the case if the accumulation within it were dredged and removed altogether; for the conservation of the harbour I strongly recommend the use of a powerful dredging machine.

"I am of opinion that by resorting to efficient dredging the depth of water at the entrance may be increased, and the accretion within the harbour removed without the aid of sluicing, and that the Bassins de Retenue de l'Ecluse Leopold, and de Française may hereafter be converted into efficient floating docks at a moderate cost."

On March 13th Mons. Devaux wrote to Sir Myles Fenton to acknowledge the receipt of this report in these words :—" I had the honour of laying before the King the report of Mr. Abernethy on the subject of dredging the entrance to the harbour at Ostend. His majesty was greatly interested with this report, and wishes that you would be so kind as to thank Mr. Abernethy on his part for his great kindness. Nothing could be better than this remarkable paper."

Several more interviews with his majesty followed, at one of which, in the month of May, the English visitors dined at the Palace. The scheme for improving Ostend Harbour was eventually approved of, but the work was never carried out, the reason assigned being want of funds owing to the great expenditure incurred in building the Palais de Justice. The project had been in contemplation for nearly ten years, and it is only fair to mention that the South-Eastern Railway Company had done all in their power to bring about the improved communication with Belgium, and in reliance upon satisfactory arrangements being forthcoming, had in the meanwhile constructed a line of railway to Port Victoria, and erected a temporary deep water pier. In 1888-90 Mr. Abernethy furnished further designs for a harbour there, and prepared

Parliamentary plans.   The Act was obtained, but
operations have not, as yet, been commenced.

In April of the year 1881, Mons. Jacquemyns, the
Belgian Minister of the Interior, addressed the following
letter to Mr. Abernethy :—

"Monsieur Abernethy, Président de la Société des Ingénieurs
de Londres.
"Monsieur,
"Le Roi des Belges a fondé un prix de vingt-cinq
mille francs, en faveur du meilleur ouvrage sur les moyens
d'améliorer les ports établis sur les côtes basses et sablonneuses
comme celles de la Belgique.

"Un très grand nombre de concurrents ont pris part a ce
concours international S. M. a l'intention de vous appeler à faire
partie du Jury qui sera chargé de décerner le prix. Je viens
vous prier, Monsieur, de vouloir bien me faire connaitre s'il entre
dans vos convenances d'accepter cette mission.

"Recevez, Monsieur, l'assurance de ma considération la plus
distinguée,
" Le Ministre de l'Interieur,
"(Signed)   G. Rolin Jacquemyns.
"Bruxelles, 18 Avril, 1881."

The invitation was accepted, and the gentlemen of
the jury to award the prize were :—

"MM. D'Elhoungne, Ministre d'Etat, Membre de la Chambre,
des Représentants, Président.

"Michel, Inspecteur Général de la Marine.

"Symon, Ingénieur en Chef, Directeur des Ponts et Chaussées.

"Abernethy, Président de la Société des Ingénieurs Civils de
Londres.

"Dirks, Ingénieur en Chef du Waterstaat à Amsterdam.

"Lyster, Ingénieur en Chef, des Docks à Liverpool.

"Plocq, Ingénieur en Chef des Ponts et Chausées à Boulogne-sur-Mer.

Fifty-three Competition Papers were sent in, and the Jury ultimately found as follows :—

"Résumant son opinion sur le mémoire de M. Demey, le Jury constate que l'auteur a fait preuve, non seulement d'une science très étendue et d'une grande profondeur de vue dans l'etude du régime des côtes, mais encore d'un esprit très pratique et d'une prudence très louable dans les solutions qu'il préconise pour l'amélioration des ports. Si ce mémoire ne contient pas beaucoup de suggestions absolument nouvelles, le Jury ne croit pas devoir lui en faire un reproche : il vaut mieux, à ses yeux, dans une question aussi difficile et aussi complexe que celle soumise au concours, s'en tenir aux données positives qui résultent de la science et des faits acquis, que de s'aventurer dans des conceptions téméraires. Il y a lieu de remarquer d'ailleurs que quelques-unes des solutions recommandées par l'auteur étaient nouvelles en 1880, quand il les présentait, et se sont trouvées justifiées depuis lors par la pratique.

"En conséquence, le Jury a attribué le prix du Roi à M. Demey. Cette décision a été adoptée à l'unanimité moins une voix."

Six years later, on April 2nd, 1887, His Majesty was graciously pleased to confer upon Mr. Abernethy the honour of Commander of the Order of Leopold, for his services as a member of the Jury, in inspecting the designs, and awarding the prize.

HULL.

1880-5.

FOR many years past Hull has been classed as
the third port in the United Kingdom, London
and Liverpool taking precedence as first and second
respectively, but until the execution of the works
authorised by the Hull and Barnsley and West
Riding Junction Railway and Dock Act, in 1882,
Hull possessed but one direct means of communication with the adjoining inland manufacturing towns,
viz: by the North Eastern Railway. Although, too,
the town had the advantage of being situated in close
proximity to the South Yorkshire coalfields, with the
great natural facilities of its river Humber, two and a
half miles wide, which rendered it accessible to the
largest class of vessels at low water, it was not a coal
port in the sense of that commodity being its pre-

dominent export. The principal reason, no doubt,
why the coal traffic had not been hitherto more
strenuously cultivated by vessels frequenting the port,
was that its cost and the delay in its despatch were
enhanced by the prevailing conditions of railway tran-
sit from the collieries, coupled with the inadequate
dock accommodation afforded, and inefficiency of the
appliances for its shipment. Railway and dock accommodation had remained singularly neglected. Previous
attempts had certainly been made to bring about an
increase in trade, but they had been spasmodic and
lacked cohesion of interest. Schemes for docks and
railways as independent enterprises under separate
management, had been launched, but unsuccessfully.
Hull was still keeping her position as the third commercial port in the kingdom, but was making no
advance : and to maintain one's ground only, and do
no more, is, in these days of active competition, virtually
to lose it.

Realizing this position of affairs, several of the
leading citizens, headed by Lieut.-Colonel Gerard
Smith, C.B., now Governor of Western Australia,
came to Parliament in the Session of 1880, with a
bold and comprehensive scheme, to make a direct
line to the South Yorkshire coalfields, near Barnsley,
together with a deep water dock at Hull, and the Bill
then thrown out was reintroduced two years later and

passed after two protracted parliamentary battles
of almost unexampled severity, and at an expense of
£115,000. The design of this dock was entrusted to
Mr. Abernethy, and during its construction he was
assisted by Messrs. Oldham and Bohn, civil engineers
of Hull, while Mr. A. C. Hurtzig acted as resident
engineer throughout. This magnificent dock, called
after H.R.H. the Princess of Wales, the Alexandra
Dock, was finished and opened on July 16th, 1885.
It has an area of 46½ acres, being 2,300 feet in length,
and 1,000 feet in breadth, and is nearly twice the size
of the Albert Dock at Hull. As a preliminary operation, about 150 acres of land were first reclaimed
from the Humber by embanking, so that it is situated
on what was formerly the foreshore of that river.

The sea bank which was formed to exclude the water
from the dock works, is one and a quarter mile in
length, composed of 200,000 tons of chalk, and faced
with Bramley Fall stone, with a slope of 2 to 1 on the
sea face, while the cofferdam built across the entrance
to the lock during construction, was 500 feet in length,
and on a curve with a radius of 256 feet. It was
composed of two rows of piles, in number about 1,000,
and varying in length from 50 feet to 60 feet, driven
6 feet apart, and the intermediate space filled in with
puddled clay. The lock is approached from the river
through a trumpet-shaped entrance 360 feet in width,

with a timber wharf, 300 feet long on either side.
These wharves are built on piles of creosoted timber, 60 feet long. The lock measures 550 feet in
length and 85 feet in width, with a depth of 34 feet
over the sill at high water ordinary spring tides, and
has three pairs of massive Demarara greenheart gates.
The principal features of the dock are its accessibility
to large vessels at all times, and its large quay space
of two miles, of which a considerable proportion is
occupied by one railway jetty, three jetties built of
masonry projecting from the outer wall towards the
centre one on the west, two more on the south side,
and the large water space, which affords anchorage
for vessels waiting for a cargo, and so enables other
vessels for which cargoes are ready, to occupy the
loading berths, and the work of loading to be carried
on uninterruptedly. The walls of the dock are 40
feet 6 inches high from ground level, their depth
below that point varying from 10 feet to 15 feet, according to the nature of their foundation, and are 20 feet
wide at the base, and 6 feet 9 inches at the top. They
are composed of chalk rubble masonry, faced with
ashlar, and finished with a granite coping, and at
the north-east side are two graving docks, one 500
feet by 60 feet by 19 feet, and the other 550 feet by
65 feet by 21½ feet, and the dock is filled and supplied
with fresh water from a land stream, known as the

Holderness Drain, and in that way the expense of
dredging is saved, a process which cost the old Dock
Company £10,000 per annum, in consequence of the
mud which is deposited by the admission of the water
from the Humber.

Some idea of the magnitude of the work involved in
the construction of the Alexandra Dock, which was
admirably done by the well known firm of contractors,
Messrs. Lucas & Aird, at an actual cost of £1,355,392,
or £29,147 per acre, including equipment, may be
gathered from the appended figures of what was
actually done for the money, and the amount of the
plant in use.

DESCRIPTION.	QUANTITY.	
Excavation	3,350,000	cubic yards
Dredging	661,000	,,
Limestone	50,000	tons
Cement	14,000	,,
Sand and gravel	400,000	,,
Mortar	70,000	cubic yards
Lime concrete	74,000	,,
Cement concrete	88,000	,,
Chalk rubble masonry ...	144,000	,,
Bramley Fall masonry ...	136,000	,,
Brickwork	15,000	,,
Granite	115,000	cubic feet
Dressed Bramley Fall ashlar	349,000	,,

DESCRIPTION.	QUANTITY.
Rock faced Bramley Fall ashlar	608,000 cubic feet
Timber, in piles and sheeting	390,000 ,,
Timber, in walings, bracings, etc.	92,000 ,,
Chalk stone embankment ...	293,000 cubic yards
Timber used in temporary ... work	1,500,000 cubic feet
Coal	60,000
Locomotives used	31
Wagons and trucks	975
Moveable engines	37
Cranes	42
Pile engines	24
Steam navvies	5
Hydraulic navvies	2
Boilers under steam ...	150
Men (greatest number at any time employed)	3,500

All the hydraulic machinery in connection with the lock gates, etc., was designed and supplied by Sir W. Armstrong, Mitchell & Co., and the machinery for loading and unloading exports and imports, was supplied by the same firm, and is also hydraulic. The exports at Hull, other than coal, are chiefly goods of great value in proportion to their bulk—agricultural machinery, cotton and wollen manufactures, and the like; while the imports are mainly heavy goods, such as grain, timber, seeds, etc.

It is worthy of note that in the course of constructing the Alexandra Dock at Hull, hydraulic power was for the first time applied to working the excavators. Two of the six excavators or navvies was worked by this power: an hydraulic crane put the stonework at the dock walls in place, while an hydraulic jigger raised the barrows laden with soil from the bottom of the dock to the wall. This machinery was found to work at least as quickly, as easily, and as economically as steam machinery, and it had the advantage of doing so almost without noise, and quite without smoke.

BOSTON.

1881-4.

DURING the construction of the Alexandra Dock
at Hull, Mr. Abernethy was also acting as
consulting engineer to the new dock at Boston, the
designs for which had been prepared by Mr. W. H.
Wheeler, M.I.C.E., who also superintended the work
throughout. The port, which is situated on the mouth
of the river Witham, shortly before it reaches the
Wash on the east coast, was at one time one of the
chief places for the import and export of goods from
Flanders and the Low Countries. Large quantities of
wine from the Rhine and Elbe for the use of the
monasteries, and merchandise from the Continent
were delivered at Boston and Lynn; while corn, wood,
leather, and other goods were exported in return.
But from the fourteenth century it began to decline as a

o

commercial port, its trade being diverted to other places,
though a considerable trade remained till the increased
draught of ships, difficulties of navigation, and the
want of floating accommodation, had nearly reduced
it to the condition of an inland town. In 1880 an
Act of Parliament was obtained for improving the
outfall of the Witham, which being obliged hitherto
to find its way to the Wash through a mass of shifting
sands, afforded a very imperfect discharge, and in
times of heavy rainfall the lands were constantly
flooded. The Outfall Board was constituted of representatives from the Witham Drainage and Black
Sluice Trust, the two principal drainage systems, and
the Boston Harbour Commissioners. A new cut,
about three miles in length, was commenced from the
point where the harbour authorities' previous improvements in training the river had ceased, and extended
into deep water as advised in 1793, and subsequently
by Mr. Rennie and Sir John Hawkshaw. This cut
is 130 feet wide at the bottom with slopes of 4½ to 1,
and has 27 feet of water at high water of ordinary
spring tides, the width of the top of the cutting, which
is level with ordinary high water, being 300 feet.

This improvement of the Witham, rendered feasible
the construction of a dock at Boston, and from its
geographical position as the nearest port to the coalfields of Nottinghamshire and Derbyshire on the one

side, and the Continent on the other, it is well situated
for the export of coals, salt, machinery, etc., and the
import of timber, grain, and agricultural produce, in
return.

The Corporation of the town in their capacity of
Harbour Commissioners, obtained the Act to make
the dock in 1881, the money to be raised on the
security of the harbour tolls and borough revenue. In
the House of Lords, the Bill was strongly opposed by
the Ocean Dock Company, who in the same Session
were promoting a Bill for a dock lower down the river,
but the Boston Dock Bill passed, and work was
commenced in 1882. This consisted of a dock 825 feet
long by 450 feet at the widest end, the area being nearly
seven acres; a lock 300 feet by 50 feet, with two pairs
of gates, the depth of water at the sill at ordinary
spring tides being 25 feet, excavation and dredging of
the bank at its entrance, a swing bridge 126 feet long
across the river to connect the dock with the goods
yard of the Great Northern Railway, and two miles of
line. The dock walls are 32 feet 6 inches in height
from the toe to the coping; 13 feet 6 inches thick at
the base, and 6 feet at the top, having a batter on the
face of 1 in 4 for the first 10 feet above the floor, and
1 in 16 for the upper part, and were constructed of
concrete formed of 5 parts of burnt clay ballast, 1 part
of sand, 2 of sea shingle, to 1 of Portland cement.

As the concrete was deposited, rough blocks of concrete stone, as taken from the quarries near Sleaford, were embedded, the quantity forming one-fourth of the whole mass, no stone being allowed to be near the face or within 6 inches of another stone. The foundations and braces of the lock were made of similar concrete to that employed in the dock walls, but in the case of the lock, the walls were faced throughout with Staffordshire blue bricks, the blocks of brickwood for the facing being alternately, 1 foot 6 inches and 3 feet, while the sill and hollow quoins were of Cornish granite. The dock gates were built of pitch pine with green-heart heel mitre posts and bottom ribs, each gate measuring 29 feet 6 inches in length, 32 feet in height, and 2 feet 7 inches in depth at the lowest part. Mr. C. D. W. Parker, C.E., was resident engineer during the principal part of the time, when he obtained an appointment at the Hull Docks, and was succeeded by Mr. R. J. Allen, C.E.

THE MANCHESTER SHIP CANAL.

1880-93.

THE greatest engineering work with which Mr.
Abernethy was professionally connected, and
which he lived to see completed, was the Manchester
Ship Canal. Any serious attempt to give a description
of the vast number of " works of art " throughout the
canal's length of thirty-six miles from Manchester to
Eastham, its lofty viaducts and bridges over which the
deviated lines of railway now pass, the swing bridges
to enable masted vessels to traverse its course, the
swing aqueduct at Barton which conducts the old
Bridgewater Canal overhead, the gigantic sluices at the
Weaver mouth and elsewhere, the numerous locks and
docks, to say nothing of the less interesting portion of
the work, such as the immense extent of excavation,
walls and embankments, would require the space of

many chapters, and even if some fairly adequate account
of the different works alluded to could be abridged into a
conveniently small space, the description would still be
very imperfect, inasmuch as the great engineering
difficulties both foreseen and unforeseen which presented
themselves during the progress of the work, would
still remain unnoticed, and the services of the
engineers and contractors, beginning with Sir E. L.
Williams, the engineer-in-chief and responsible head,
downwards, upon whose skill and energy the final
triumph so much depended, and to each of whom a
share of merit is in all justice due, would also be
awaiting recognition.   Fortunately an accurate description of the entire undertaking when completed may
be found in the special number of " Engineering,"
published on January 26th, 1894, and the names of
those whose services called for special mention may
there be found also.

Accordingly it is proposed in the present chapter
to refer only to the part which Mr. Abernethy took in
this historic work, and for the purpose the description
referred to also lends valuable assistance

It was in 1880 that Mr. Daniel Adamson, who
together with Mr. Hicks had conceived the project of
forming a waterway to Manchester, first came to London to consult him with regard to the scheme, and the
upshot of the interview was, that the engineer expressed

his willingness to follow up the idea and assist to the
best of his ability, provided that some influential Manchester gentlemen could be found to support and pro-
secute the scheme. Two years later, in 1882, a
Provisional Committee was formed to consider two
projects for effecting the waterway, one submitted by
the late Mr. Hamilton Fulton, C.E., who advocated a
tidal channel up to Manchester, and the other by Mr.
(now Sir) E. Leader Williams, who proposed a canal
from Manchester to Runcorn, and thence seaward by
the River Mersey. These two rival schemes were submitted by the Provisional Committee to Mr. Abernethy
for consideration and opinion, and after inspecting the
Rivers Irwell and Mersey from Manchester to Runcorn,
he reported in favour of the plans put forward by Sir E.
Leader Williams. The tenor of his report was adopted,
and he was further requested to act as consulting
engineer, and in that capacity advised and gave
evidence in support of the Bills before Parliament in
the Sessions of 1883, 1884, and 1885. Upon the rejection of Mr. Fulton's scheme by the Provisional Committee, Sir E. L. Williams remained in possession of
the field, and a vast field it proved, not only in point of
area, but for the exercise of exceptional ability, energy,
and tact, all of which qualities were in constant demand
in order to bring the undertaking to a successful issue.
But the Bill brought forward in 1883 proposed a very

different work to that finally authorized in the Session
of 1885. As originally designed, the main entrance to
the canal was to be at Runcorn, and from thence to
Garston a channel was to be dredged, and kept open by
means of half-tide training walls. The canal was to
have a depth of 22 feet, and to be 100 feet in width.
The first of the three locks was to be at Latchford,
between which point and Manchester the old river was
to be completely canalized, much in the same manner
as has since been carried out, and there were to be
docks at Latchford, Irlam, and Barton, as well as the
terminal docks at Manchester. But a departure from
the scheme as originally designed was made even
before the first application to Parliament, in so far that
instead of utilizing the existing river channel to War-
rington, the river bed was to be abandoned about 1½
mile above Runcorn, and a new cutting mainly depended
upon. The Bill for 1883 was duly deposited in the
preceding November, but a serious omission to comply
with the requirements of Standing Orders jeopardised
its existence at an early stage ; upon petition, however,
the House of Commons waived the Standing Orders in
its favour, and so saved the Bill in the only way in which
it could be saved, and in due time it came before a
Committee of the House. Thirty-seven days were
occupied in discussion, at the end of which time it
was passed, but saddled with conditions which entailed

a further application to Parliament in a subsequent
Session. The promoters, however, thought fit to proceed to the House of Lords, but unfortunately the
Special Committee of Peers took a different view, and
declined to allow a Bill to proceed which would in part
depend upon a another yet to be obtained.

But the temporary reverse only had the effect of
arousing the energy of the promoters, and inciting them
all the more keenly to prepare for the following Session,
and in 1884 a second Bill, similar in its main features
to the first, came on for hearing. But there were
several important alterations. The locks were to be
brought lower down, training walls were to be made
down to Garston, at which point they were to be 1000
feet wide, diminishing to 400 feet opposite the River
Weaver, whence the channel would gradually close
into the canal proper. It was in opposition to
this proposed estuary work that the main evidence of
the opponents was directed. Would the effect of these
training walls diminish the tidal flow in the Mersey?
was the great question which the Committee were
called upon to decide.

The estuary of the Mersey is narrower near the
entrance than in the upper portion, and the tide naturally
runs harder where the sectional area is less, and so
keeps the channel clear by scour. The Mersey Docks
and Harbour Board said, and said legitimately, and

were supported in their contention by strong engineering evidence, that if the upper portion of the estuary
were interfered with by constructing these training
walls, the shoals would increase, less water would ebb
and flow, the tidal scour diminish, and finally the
channel over the bar silt up.

In that year the contest began in the Upper House
and the Bill passed, but the Lower House refused its
sanction, so no headway was as yet made, and the
scheme remained to be brought forward and contested
in a future Session.

At this juncture the Provisional Committee again
asked the advice of their consulting engineer, and he
reported to them in favour of an alternative design,
viz., a canal independently of the tideway from Manchester to Eastham, and at the earliest opportunity, in
the Session of 1885, the promoters introduced their Bill
by which the estuary works were eliminated.   To
Mr. G. F. Lyster, the late engineer to the Mersey
Docks and Harbour Board, the credit is due of having
made this practical suggestion while giving evidence in
the preceding year in opposition to the proposed estuary
works, and the promoters now embodied the suggestion
in their Bill, and so got free from a strong element of
opposition.   But even with this relief given, thirty
days were consumed in the House of Lords, and thirty-
five more in the House of Commons before the great

scheme passed through both Houses.   It was, however this time, under the able pilotage of Mr. Pember, Q C., the leading counsel, conducted safely through its two long voyages, and received the Royal Assent and so became an Act in 1885 and an accomplished fact in 1894, but it is stated that the actual expenditure incurred in obtaining the authority to commence the work amounted to £350,000.

At this stage the appointment of consulting engineer was renewed, and he undertook to visit and inspect the work while in course of construction once in every month and report its progress and condition to the Works Committee.   This duty he continued to perform until 1893, when the canal was nearly completed, its success from a constructive point of view assured, and his services no longer required.   It was informally opened for traffic on January 1st, 1894, and formally by Her Majesty the Queen on May 21st of the same year. The cost of construction was over £13,500,000.

His association with the Manchester Ship Canal, however, which had in every sense been a memorable and pleasant one from first to last, was sadly changed after its completion by the death of his son Harold, who had throughout the undertaking acted under Sir E. L. Williams as resident engineer upon the difficult Runcorn section, and had had charge of the construction during the first three years of seven, and afterwards of ten miles of the canal. Shortly before the opening in January, 1894, he contracted a malarial fever upon the canal works, which at intervals incapacitated him from work, and gradually assuming a more malignant form, culminated in his death at the age of thirty-six on his way home from Cape Town, whither he had gone for a sea voyage on July 9th, 1895. He had previously done much good work as assistant engineer at Hull, and at Lake Aboukir in Egypt.

FRASERBURGH,

1857—96.

ONE more harbour work of importance remains to be mentioned, and that is Fraserburgh, the chief Scottish port of the herring fishery, some fifty miles north of Aberdeen.

It is just forty years since the engineer whose career has been given in this Biography, was first consulted with reference to Fraserburgh Harbour, and although this long association would naturally suggest the propriety of an earlier mention, it appears to occupy a more appropriate place in the book as last on the special list, inasmuch as the advice given in 1857 has only within the past two years been fully carried out, and also because it was the last work upon which he was actually engaged.

In the year 1857 he recommended to the Harbour

Commissioners an extension of the Balaclava East
Pier, built in 1851, in an easterly direction, by forming
a breakwater 720 feet in length, reaching to the further
edge of the Outer Bush Rock, with a view to sheltering
the Balaclava and North Harbours. Sixteen years
later, in 1873 a Provisional Order was obtained in
order to carry out the recommendations of the report,
and a loan of £60,000 was granted by the Public
Works' Loan Commission for the construction of the
works. These comprised a breakwater, extending east-
south-east for 680 feet, and then turning south-east for
180 feet, and terminating on the outer Bush Rock, and
the widening of the Balaclava East Pier, on the sea
side, to the extent of 16½ feet along its entire length
of 1400 feet, so as to give width for a roadway to
convey materials to the breakwater without encroaching
upon the quay space or reducing the area of the basin.
As the breakwater was to be exposed to the heavy
seas raised by north and north-east gales, it was
designed to be formed of a solid mass of concrete in
position above low water, 30 feet wide, and having its
quay 10 feet above high water protected by a parapet
9½ feet high. Mr. J. H. Bostock, M.I.C.E., carried
out the work, as resident engineer. The widening
of the Balaclava Pier, the first of the two works
executed under the loan, was commenced at the end of
1875, and completed in October, 1877, and contains

15,300 cubic yards of concrete. The breakwater, begun
in the spring of 1878, was completed in the autumn of
1882. It consisted of 15,274 cubic yards of concrete
in bags, and 25,106 cubic yards of concrete in position,
or a total of 40,380 cubic yards, and the total cost of
the works amounted to £69,000. Thus a good deal had
been done to give the harbour better protection, but
much that had been advised, had to remain undone
until the Harbour Commissioners could see their way
to apply for a fresh loan. This came to pass in 1894,
when extensive works were undertaken, embracing, not
only deepening the large area of harbour four feet in the
hard rock, and the erection of jetties, but also the
deepening of the entrance to the channel, the formation
of a new breakwater at the south side, the strengthen-
ing of Balaclava Breakwater, and the building of a dry
dock, three and a half acres, the largest of its kind in
Scotland, and intended for wintering the large local
fleet of first class fishing boats. These boats have
hitherto been drawn up in winter on the piers, a process which frequently strained them, and the Harbour
Commissioners by making this provision for their
fishermen, have shown a timely consideration for them
on the first occasion when it has been in their power
to do so.

At the time of Mr. Abernethy's death, a portion
only of these additional works had been regarded as

likely to be carried out in the near future, but all of them have since been undertaken and completed after considerable difficulties in the early stage, owing to extensive "blows" through the North Pier, well within the estimate, and the surplus of the money advanced by the Public Loan Commissioners on the security of the rates, which remained over after their completion, has been devoted to building the dry dock. Some four years since he took his two elder sons into partnership, and Mr. G. N. Abernethy has continued to carry on this work to its successful termination. Mr. G. Fitzgibbon has, since operations began in 1894, acted as the resident engineer at Fraserburgh, and has most ably superintended the carrying out of a difficult engineering work. The harbour space is now thirty-eight acres, with a mile and a half of quays, and all the necessary facilities for the landing and curing of fish. The navigation and harbour works may be pronounced complete, but the fish market so much required remains to be built. This the inhabitants of Fraserburgh, who have done so much for their harbour during the past twenty years, and are now deservedly benefiting by the increased trade resulting from their enterprise, have decided to erect as soon as possible.

The Aberdeen Journal of April 12th of this year, in speaking of the work nearly finished, said :—

FRASERBURGH, JUNE, 1895.

To face page 209.

"The scheme of improvement planned forty years ago, by the late Mr. James Abernethy, is now nearing completion, and the work has already been fully justified by the results, both from an engineering and a financial point of view. The scheme projected by the eminent engineer has produced the desired effect, and the growth of the portal revenue by 100 per cent. within twenty years, may be regarded as a further proof of the well known principle, that where facilities are provided traffic will certainly follow."

The cost of the last built works has been £82,000. Messrs. Price and Wills, of Westminster, undertook the contract, and executed it within the engineers' estimate, and in a manner which has given universal satisfaction. The accompanying plate shows a portion of the Balaclava Harbour laid dry, and certain of their staff in possession of the premises. The harbour entrance has been enclosed by a cofferdam in the autumn of each of the past years till the following July, the water pumped out, and operations continued ; while in July of each year the cofferdam has been removed, the sea admitted, and the herring fishery briskly carried on as usual, and with the advantage each season of the deepened portions of the harbour which had been effected before the re-admission of water.

A CIRCUIT OF ENGLAND AND WALES—AND OF IRELAND.

WITH the description of the improvements recently effected in the harbour of Fraserburgh, it is thought that a sufficiently long list of more important engineering works, undertaken and sucessfully completed, has been given, to enable the reader to form an independent judgment as to the utility of the life reviewed. It will have been noted that Mr. Abernethy's long professional career was spent mainly in the furtherance of one particular branch of civil engineering, namely, harbours and docks, and that by applying himself to that branch, and having the good fortune to be appointed as engineer to carry out such works, and thereby acquire the necessary experience, he had, at a comparatively early age, reached a position of some distinction as a specialist. He was possibly aided in achieving an early success by the circumstance of the majority of the leading engineers of the day devoting themselves to the construction of railways, a new department of civil engineering which opened out in the first quarter of the present century, and increased with startling rapidity during the reign of William the Fourth, and the first few years after Her Majesty had ascended the Throne, and which, to a large extent, diverted the attention of the profession. With the prospect of a large amount of work to be done in the near future, in consequence of this new adaptation of steam power, the majority of the younger engineers were also borne away with the current known as the "railway mania," and thus he may, to some extent, have been relieved from competition with many men of ability of equal standing, who would otherwise have proved formidable rivals in the special branch of the science which he had selected to follow up.

The tendency towards specialization in any given science can be traced back for a long period, and it is one that has steadily increased. Pope recognised its value and certain future in the lines :—

> "One science only will one genius fit,
> So vast is art, so narrow human wit,
> Not only bounded by peculiar arts,
> But oft in these confined to single parts."

and the selection of harbours and docks as special

subjects, was by no means an unfortunate one sixty years ago. For as "all returning rivers run towards the sea," so in conformance with the law laid down by Nature, the majority of railways in this country lead down to the coast, and it is there that the hydraulic engineers' services are required.

But whatever circumstances may have combined to assist him in making a good start, to himself alone must be attributed the credit of having thenceforward maintained and steadily improved the position he had so early won, and for having done this in a manner which commended itself to brother engineers and thereby earned their respect. The secret of the ultimate success of his numerous works seems to be contained in drawing a correct line of demarcation between theory and practice, and while always willing to accept the former, at the same time, never to do so before applying some previous test to ascertain its possible value, and ever bearing in mind that :

> " Nature like art is but restrained,
> By the same laws which first herself ordained."

Mr. Abernethy's first important work was, as has been already stated, at his native city Aberdeen, and his last at Fraserburgh, some forty-seven miles further north in the same county, and during the interval of fifty-six years he had practically completed a circuit of work around the coast line of Great Britain.

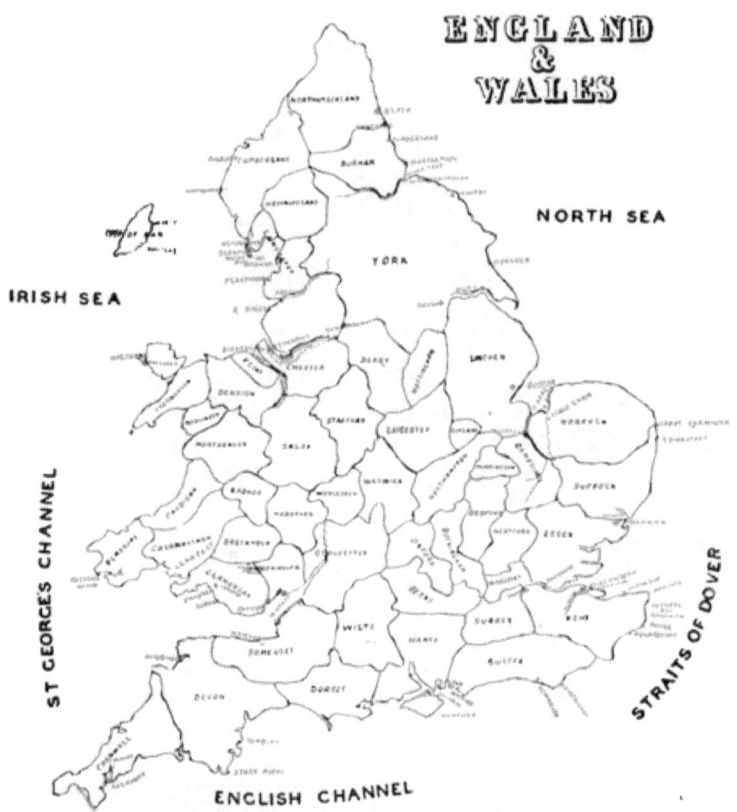

To face page 213.

On the Western and Northern shores of Scotland few schemes of importance have been projected during the long interval, and consequently his scenes of operations in those parts are few and far between, though it may be here mentioned that for several years he acted on behalf of the Clyde Trustees; but on the Eastern coast at Leith, Dundee, and even the far off Wick, his advice has at times been solicited, and given in the form of reports.

It was on the shores of England and Wales, however, that his chief scenes of work are located and in order to avoid the tedium which would be likely to attend an exhaustive enumeration of the seaport towns at which he has been engaged, the accompanying map has been prepared with the intention of conveying the same information at a glance, and so perhaps in more acceptable form, to the reader. Each harbour on the coast at which his professional services have, in the author's judgment, been of sufficient consequence to warrant the association of his name with it, will there be seen marked in red letters, and the illustration will, it is hoped, bear out and substantiate the statement of his having completed a circuit of the entire coast line of England and Wales.

Many of the places mentioned on the map there make their first and last appearance in this book, but they suggest much additional useful work, though perhaps not of sufficient importance or interest as to call for special mention. In a few instances the places marked in red have reference to schemes designed only and not executed, as docks at Dagenham, at Tranmere near Birkenhead, and at Heysham near Morecombe, for the Midland Railway Company, the last named project however, will shortly be commenced by Messrs. J. A. McDonald and G. N. Abernethy, members of the Institution of Civil Engineers.

There is no engineering work of consequence to record in connection with London, and therefore it has not been marked on the map. But from another point of view it should have been written in large type, for Westminster had been the centre of his business since 1854, and for the last forty years of his life he had acquired a large additional practice there as a consulting engineer, especially in supporting or opposing Engineering Bills before Parliamentary Committees.

The omission of London further seems to increase in gravity when it is remembered that in 1882-4 he served as a member of the Royal Commission on Metropolitan Sewage Discharge, of which the late Lord Bramwell was Chairman, his fellow Commissioners being, the late Sir John Coode, C.E., Sir P. Benson Maxwell, Prof. A. W. Williamson, F.R.S., Col. C. B. Ewart, C.B. R.E., and Messrs. F. S. B. de Chaumont, F.R.S., and Thomas Stevenson, M.D. Meetings were held for the examination of witnesses on sixty different occasions, extending over a period of two and a quarter years, and an elaborate first report was presented on January 31st, 1884, and a second and final report on November 27th of the same year.

But it may be asked by some readers, what has he done for Ireland? The answer is, nothing of much importance, but something, and that he would have liked to have done more if the opportunity had been given. The "something" consists mainly in having acted as a Member of the Royal Commission on Irish Public Works in the years 1886 and 1887, in conjunction with the late Sir James Allport, Managing Director of the Midland Railway Company, Messrs. J. Wolfe Barry, K.C.B., Pres. Inst. C.E., and J. Todhunter Pim of Dublin, with Mr. S. E. Spring Rice as Secretary, and having as a member of that Commission been a party to recommending certain improvements for the welfare of that country, some of which have been since effected by the Government.

The subjects entrusted to the Royal Commissioners for enquiry were principally three: 1. Deep Sea Fisheries; 2. Arterial Drainage; 3. Railway Extension and Organization. To the second of these headings, which stated more fully, involved an enquiry as to "what measures are required with due regard to the improvement or preservation of any necessary

facilities for inland navigation, for the completion and
maintenance of the system of arterial drainage in
Ireland, especially in the districts of the Shannon, the
Barrow, and the Bann," the Commissioners directed
their attention first, and reported that the catchment
area of every river as far as the limit of tidal water,
should be put in the charge of a separate body of conservators, to be composed of representatives of the
various interests concerned, who were to be held responsible for the maintenance and improvement of the main
watercourses, and who were to have the necessary
powers given to them for executing works, and obtaining funds.

The composition of the Board of Conservators would
accordingly as recommended, consist of representatives
of the lands benefited, the catchment area, the towns,
and the Government Drainage Department.

Commencing with the River Shannon, the first and
finest river in Ireland, the Commissioners suggested
certain controlling works in the form of sluices, and the
use of Lough Allen as an impounding reservoir, and
advised the abandonment of the navigation of the river
above Athlone and the utilization of its various locks
for discharging flood waters, and that the Government
should contribute towards these works. For the River
Barrow, the upper portion of which is more subject to
floods than any other Irish river, though the lower

portion owing to a more rapid fall, and the height of its banks, is more fortunately situated, controlling works were also advocated. The removal of portions of piers and shoals which impeded the current, deepening the river bed at stated places, and the formation of embankments with back drains, were also deemed advisable.

In the case of the River Bann similar regulating works were advocated, the river bed was to be deepened, and certain sluices erected, and the Government were asked to authorize an outlay of £20,000 towards the expense of improvement. Having sent in a report upon "Arterial Drainage," dated April 9th, 1887, they proceeded to investigate the two remaining subjects, Deep Sea Fishing, and Railway Extension and Organization.

Deep Sea Fishing, an expression which is defined in the second report of the Commissioners as meaning "sea fishing which is carried on at a considerable distance from land and in deep water," was a less difficult subject of enquiry.

It was found that some 1900 boats were engaged in this industry, about 400 of this number regularly and exclusively, but that a more general use of decked sailing boats of larger tonnage was advisable. Many of the boats then in use were only eighteen to twenty feet in length, and undecked, or rowing boats of

various sizes down to the primitive "curragh," made
of tarred canvas stretched over a wooden framework.
The inferiority of the gear and nets, and the defective
local knowledge possessed by the fishermen of the fishing
grounds were also minor points noticed but deemed
of sufficient importance to call for mention in the
Report.

In many of the naturally protected harbours, such as
the Cove of Cork, Berehaven, Lough Swilly and others,
it was reported that there were no proper facilities
for landing cargoes, and that frequently such harbours
were inconveniently situated with regard to the fisher-
folk and fishing grounds.   In these natural harbours too,
piers were much required, and in districts where no
natural shelter existed, harbour accommodation was
needed.   In the case of existing Fishing Stations much
had already been done by State Agency.   For by 9 and
10 Vict. c. 3 (1846), the Government had been em-
powered to make free grants to the extent of £5000
upon any such one harbour, the balance being provided
by a loan charged either on the county, the district,
or the proprietors of adjacent lands, according to
the character and extent of the benefit conferred, in
respect of general advantages as well as regards sea
fisheries, the invitations in making application for
such assistance being left to the locality interested.
Such works when completed remained vested in the

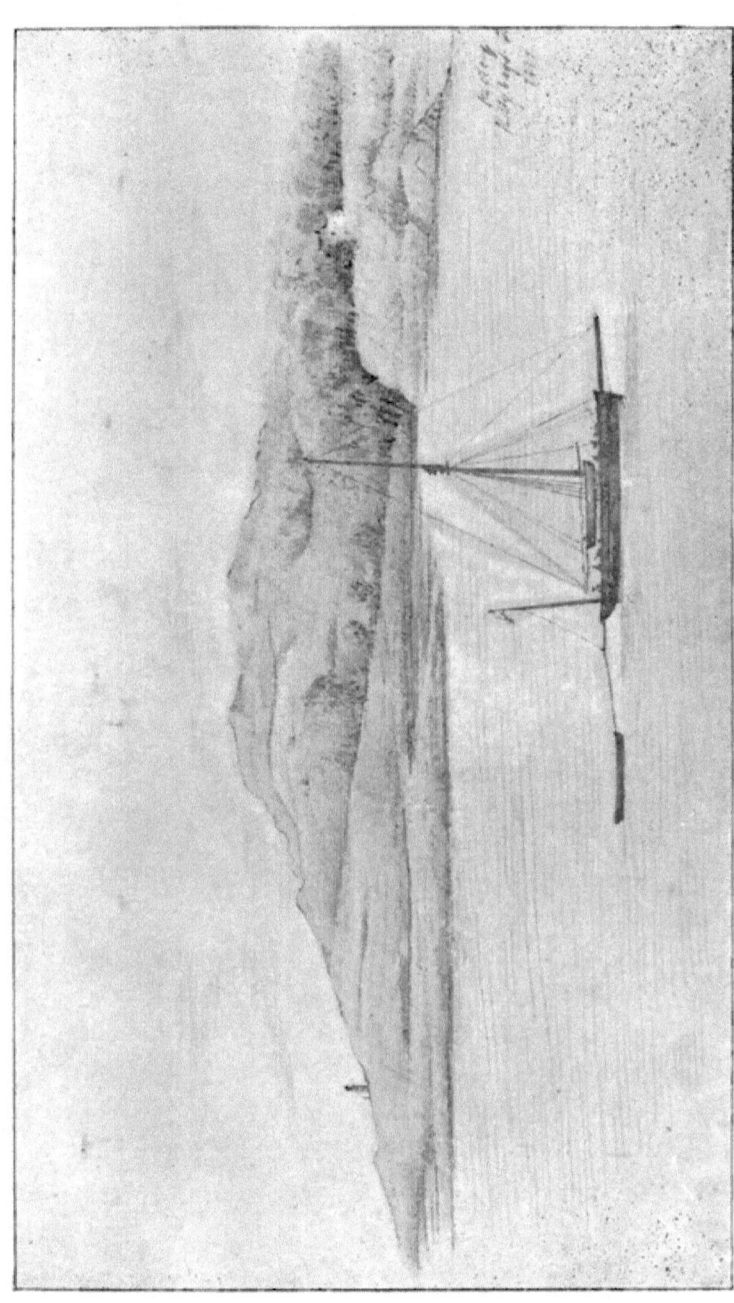

To *face page* 218.

NEAR KILLYBEGS. CO. DONEGAL, 1887.

Government, and were to be maintained out of the tolls received for their use.

But not only were the places and means of landing fish found to be defective, but there was a great want of facilities for bringing the fish to market when landed, by sea, road, or rail. The last named was clearly the best means, provided that the physical convenience were accompanied by moderation of rates.

Under the heading of "Railway Extension" to afford these facilities several lines were recommended as Downpatrick to Ardglass and the Mulroy Bay and Sheep Haven Railway, alternative lines to Killibegs, Ballina to Belmullet, and Galway to Clifden.

They advised also the connection by rail of Tralee with Dingle, Killorglin with Valencia, and Skibbereen with Baltimore, a branch line at Kinsale Harbour, and two short lines at Bantry and Dungarvan.

The second report was issued on January 4th, 1888, and several of the recommendations have since been adopted, more especially providing additional facilities for the fishing industry.

In order to obtain information respecting the three subjects submitted, enquiries were held by the Commissioners at various towns in Ireland, and witnesses examined, and in the month of June, 1887, H.M.S. "Enchantress," under the command of Captain Vine, R.N., was placed at their disposal, and on the 1st

of that month they started from Kingstown on a
four weeks cruise to inspect the harbours upon the
Irish coast.   This brief period sufficed to complete the
circuit of Ireland, in effecting which the log registered
a voyage of 1941 miles.

In a letter of June 26th 1887, after referring to a
visit of the Commissioners to Donegal on the 21st
inst., and holding a enquiry there, he wrote: "We
returned to the 'Enchantress' at Killibegs, which was
anchored in front of the town in deep water and under
perfect shelter, and next morning being Her Majesty's
Jubilee day, Captain Vine read prayers, all the officers
and crew being in grand trim, after which the whole
crew joined with us in singing 'God Save the Queen,'
which resounded over the hills and far away.   An officer
on a revenue cutter anchored close to us, managed to
fire a royal salute in good time from the only two
pieces on board, and when night came we fired off
rockets and fireworks.   The loyal houses in the town
illuminated their windows, and the lofty hill behind
had a large bonfire blazing on its summit."   This
extract from one of his letters, which affords strong
evidence of his loyalty as a subject, serves as an
appropriate introduction to a reference to other personal qualities.   Those who knew him professionally,
are equally qualified, however, to testify to these,
and their testimony will perhaps be received with

KILLYBEGS, 1887.

To face page 220.

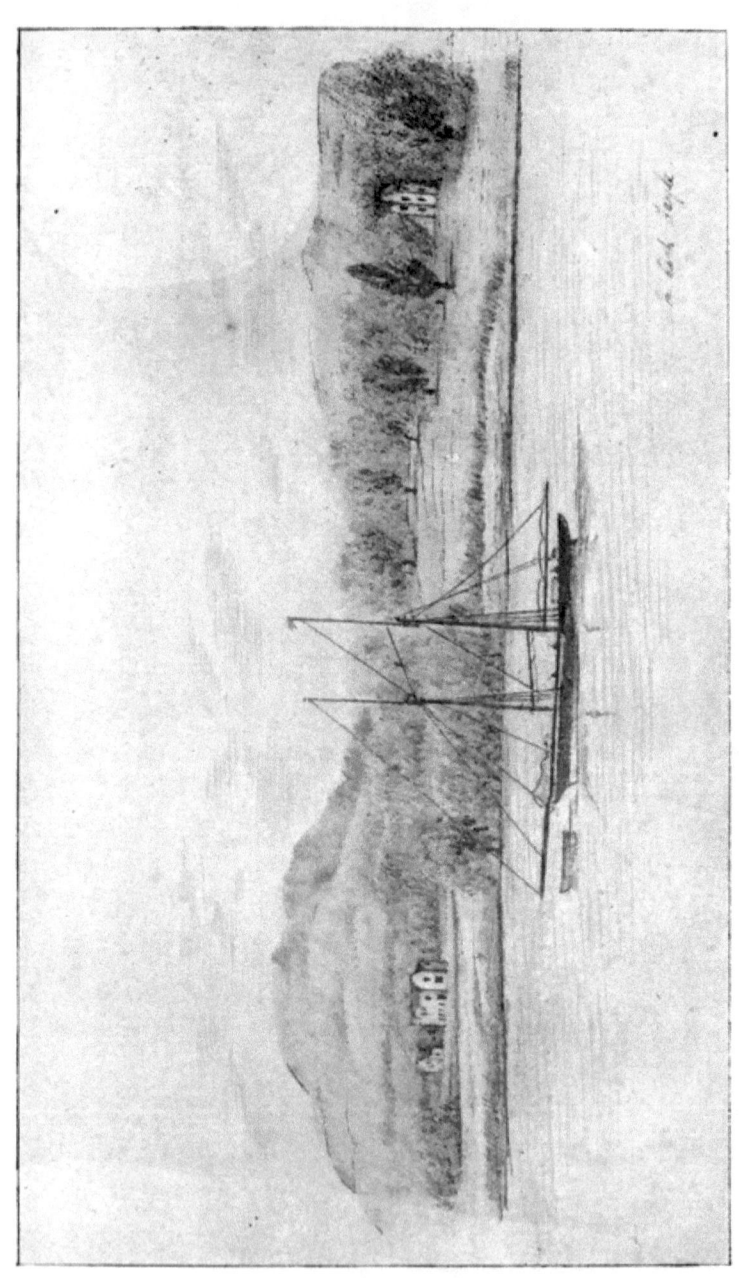

To face page 221.

SKETCH IN LOUGH FOYLE JUNE, 1887

less suspicion of partiality if they are called, instead
of his son. "Engineering" of March, 20th 1896
said of him :—"Wherever he stayed he made friends,
and everywhere he left behind him the remembrance
of his bright cheery personality, and of his goodness
of heart," and the editor of "Transport" in the issue of
March 13th, of the same year:—"With him there passed
away probably the last of the old school of harbour
engineers: and not a few of the younger men who are
now coming to the front will remember many a
kind encouragement which they have received from
Mr. Abernethy, for one of his most marked character-
istics—and this I can speak to personally—was the
almost exceptional interest he showed in the progress
of his younger brethren."

Perhaps the branch of engineering with which it has
been attempted to permanently associate his name, is
not one that appeals very forcibly to the popular
imagination, but it should be remembered that in many
instances the completion of an undertaking was in fact
a local victory gained over the sea, and that much of
his best work, by means of which a series of such
victories have been won, remains hidden either under
land or under water.

He joined the Institution of Civil Engineers in 1844
and became its President in 1881. He was also a
Fellow of the Royal Society of Edinburgh, a member

of the Society of Arts, an Associate of the Royal
Society of Naval Architects, and Justice of the Peace
for the Counties of Kent and Middlesex.   But perhaps
the most appropriate title, was that conferred upon
him in his old age by members of his own profession :
" Father of Marine Engineering."

AT HOME IN THANET.

HAVING concluded a review of his work as a civil engineer, it only remains to refer briefly to his life at home. Three houses during the past forty years would appear to possess a sufficiently good title to call for some mention as having been for several years " home ": 39, Finchley Road, St. John's Wood, facing the Swiss Cottage, from 1854 to 1865, during the greater part of which time and until the construction of the St. John's Wood Branch of the Metropolitan Railway, it bordered upon green fields and country lanes; Whiteness, Kingsgate, in Thanet, from 1863 to 1896; and 11, Prince of Wales' Terrace, Kensington, from 1863 to 1896; but it is only proposed to refer his home life as spent at one of these—the one the most enjoyed, and the one in which he died.

It was during the early autumn of the year 1859, while paying a Saturday to Monday visit to an old friend, Mr. John Dangerfield, a London solicitor, who owned one of the few houses at Kingsgate, built on a portion of the site of the once stately mansion of Henry, Lord Holland, that my father became enchanted with the wide range of sea view from the higher ground some half a mile inland, and resolved to secure it and build a country home.

" What a glorious site this would be for a country house," he exclaimed to his host, as they walked by the spot in question on the afternoon of Sunday, October 9th, 1859.

" Who would think of building a house in this exposed place," remarked the host, more in the tone of a counter exclamation than a query.

" I would, if I had the chance," was the prompt reply.

" Well," observed the host, " the farm is for sale, so you have the chance."

Upon returning from the walk the particulars of sale were obtained and examined, and George Hill Farm was, as stated, advertised for sale by auction at the " White Hart Hotel," Margate, at a near date. A business appointment at Newport, Monmouthshire, on the following day, prevented the fulfilment of his wish to immediately negotiate for the acquisition of the land, but upon his return to town on Wednesday, October 12th, he drove straight to the office of the solicitors for the property, concluded the bargain, and paid the requisite ten per cent. of the purchase money. This expeditious transaction in securing some fifty acres of bleak farm land, to which some twenty acres more have since been added, on a portion of which he had resolved to build a house, and lay out a garden, is mentioned as illustrating his quickness in forming a decision, and it may be said that an equally characteristic trait was his willingness to abide by the consequences of a judgment when once expressed.

The first impressions conveyed to his mind by the wide range and beauty of the sea view, and the thoughts of what might, with such natural advantages given, be done in the way of arboriculture to improve Nature's picture—thoughts which found expression in the remark, "what a glorious site for a country house "— were strangely different from those left upon the mind of the poet Gray, who was a visitor to the same spot in 1766. Of the particular occasion of the poet's visit we know little except that he was the guest of the Rev. William Robinson, of Denton, but he has recorded the displeasure which he felt at viewing the numerous sham ruins erected by Lord Holland in the vicinity of his house, and this may have been enough in his judgment to spoil all other surroundings. But the discrepancy

Q

between the two impressions, both quickly formed and expressed, seems to possess a certain interest from the fact that, although a long interval of time had elapsed, there had been but little change in the natural features of the locality between the two visits. A few more yards of coast line had succumbed to the incessant buffeting by the sea, and a few more trees had been planted and grown up to break the monotony of the continuous undulating corn-fields, while the locality had been rendered the more easy of access to Londoners by the extension of the South-Eastern Railway Company's system to Ramsgate and Margate. But with these changes, and all allowance for "the season's difference," the two opinions remain in strange contrast to each other.

Gray, after due time for reflection, wrote of the amenities of Kingsgate :—

> " Old and abandoned by each venal friend
>   Here Holland form'd the pious resolution
> To smuggle a few years, and strive to mend
>   A broken character and constitution.
>
> On this congenial spot he fix'd his choice
>   (Earl Godwin trembled for his neighbouring sand.)
> Here sea-gulls scream and cormorants rejoice,
>   And mariners though shipwreck'd, dread to land."

The " congenial spot " so ironically described is still fortunately enjoyed by the sea-gulls, as their presence in considerable numbers throughout the year skimming along the coast-line and uttering their harsh, weird cries as they catch sight of floating morsels of food, or tiny fish venturing dangerously near the surface, sufficiently testifies, and occasionally cormorants may still be seen to alight on the edges of the rocks when the tide is low, and outstretch their wings to dry in the same manner as their better known cousins in St. James's Park; but the mariner's risk of shipwreck has happily been reduced to a minimum by the several lightships furnished by the Trinity House of Deptford Strond, which mark by their hulls in the day time, and their variously timed occulting lights at night, the great sea highway leading to and from the Thames; while the North Foreland Lighthouse, in comparison to which the lightships seem but satellites, stands out as a " pillar of fire by night, of cloud by day."

> " And the great ships sail outward and return,
>   Bending and bowing o'er the billowy swells;
> And ever joyful as they see it burn,
>   They wave their silent welcomes and farewells."

The shipwrecked mariner's " dread to land " is an allusion to the barbarism of the inhabitants, of whom there was certainly good cause for alarm in the eighteenth century, for Lewis, in his *History of the Isle of Thanet*, 1736 (p. 34), informs us that "the sea-men here are generally reputed excellent sailors, and

show themselves very dexterous and bold in going off
to ships in distress. It is a thousand pities that they
and the country people are so apt to pilfer stranded
ships, and abuse those who have already suffered so
much. This they themselves call by the name of
Paultring, since nothing sure can be more vile and base
than, under pretence of assisting the distressed masters,
and saving theirs and the merchant's goods, to convert
them to their own use by making what they call *Guile-
shares*."

The same authority writes of Kingsgate as " a pleasant little Vill, and consisting mostly of fishermen's
houses, who get their living here by fishing, going off
to ships in distress, or carrying them fresh provisions,
beer, &c., when they pass this way on their return
from a voyage, which they call by the name of *Foying*.*
But of late it is pretty much deserted."

But the poet's irony is not yet exhausted, for he
continues :—

> " Here reign the blustering North and blighting East,
>   No tree is heard to whisper, bird to sing,
>   Yet Nature could not furnish out the feast,
>   Art he invokes, new horrors yet to bring.

* Not unfrequently during the winter months fishermen belonging to
Margate, Broadstairs, and Ramsgate, render considerable service to
vessels in distress by taking out spare anchors, chains, &c , and in
assisting stranded vessels to float off with the rising tide ; such employ-
ment and services are spoken of as " *hovelling*."

> Here mould'ring fanes and battlements arise,
>   Turrets and arches nodding to their fall,
> Unpeopled monastries delude our eyes,
>   And mimic desolation covers all."

The blustering North and blighting East still reign, and reign supreme in their season, and as to the latter wind, a resident may safely copy in his diary during the late spring for some days in advance the entry ascribed to an American, " Lat. same, Long. same, Wind same."

But the condition of things referred to in the second line of the verse were clearly capable of being changed by human agency, and much pleasure was realised in planting numerous trees and shrubs that they might be " heard to whisper and birds to sing " in close proximity to the house. Early in the spring of 1860 the services of Mr. Masters, of Canterbury, a skilful landscape gardener, were requisitioned to lay out the garden, and for the encouragement of bird life, or as the late Professor Owen expressed it, "refreshment for the orchestra," a fountain with a shallow basin was provided at which they might drink and take their morning tub.

During the summer months, especially in dry seasons, this fountain has been thronged for years with the various species of bird life in the island. The partridge, whose life is yearly becoming more precarious and his venue more restricted in this neighbourhood, will venture there in the early morning, and the coy woodpigeon at intervals during the day, after carefully reconnoitring the scene to satisfy herself that no danger is likely to attend her hurried drink. Perhaps the birds which convey to an observer the impression of deriving the greatest amount of pleasure from the proffered facilities for a bath, are starlings and wagtails, but all the passerine tribe, both residents, and summer visitors to the locality, come ceaselessly throughout the day.

For thirty-three years the late owner had the pleasure of watching the gradual growth of the garden he had made, and from time to time extended, at first visiting it in the summer months, but in recent years as frequently as professional engagements would permit, and each year as it brought an increase of growth brought with it also an additional interest in the home.

It was here on August 7th, 1888, a day of brilliant sunshine, and wholly in keeping with the occasion, he celebrated his Golden Wedding-Day, and it was not until seven years later that symptoms of failing health in his beloved life-partner first pointed to a coming dissolution of the long and happy alliance, and during the following year, 1896, they both passed peaceably away in the home they had made and been so long permitted to enjoy, death dividing them but for the short space of six months.

The energy of purpose and devotion to work which had characterised his long professional career, and which showed but little sign of having become impaired by any of the infirmities which a life of fourscore years proverbially brings in its train, was maintained during leisure hours in painting in his studio at the foot of the garden, and several of his pictures in the opinion of qualified critics bear evidence of a strong artistic talent.

With this short allusion to the country home, the author feels that his attempt to review this long career, however imperfectly performed, should close, but it is hoped that enough has been written in the pages of this small book to satisfy the reader that the life was one of the many, which have little by little but continuously, been assisting in the great progress of the country during the sixty years of Her Majesty's glorious reign, and that it has been of some marked and permanent service to mankind—as the result of an unremitting dedication both of time and talent in carrying into practical effect the aim of the Civil Engineering profession, as expressed in the words of their charter of 1824, "The Art of Directing the Great Sources of Power in Nature for the Use and Convenience of Man."

FINIS.

INDEX.

R